Because of What Happened

Because of What Happened

The Fiction Desk Anthology Series
Volume Five

Edited by Rob Redman

The Fiction Desk

First published in 2013 by The Fiction Desk Ltd.

ISBN 978-0-9567843-8-4

The Fiction Desk
PO Box 116
Rye
TN31 9DY

Please note that we do not accept postal submissions.
See our website for submissions information.

www.thefictiondesk.com

The Fiction Desk Ltd
Registered in the UK, no 07410083
Registered office: 3rd Floor, 207 Regent Street, London, W1B 3HH

Printed and bound in the UK by Imprint Digital.

Contents

Introduction

Rob Redman

Among the devices that writers use to construct a story is that great engine of cause and effect, the Machinery of Consequences, which controls and regulates much of the internal morality and logic of fiction.

By turning a lever in one direction, a writer can offer us reassurance that things happen for a reason, even for the right reason: villainy leads to punishment, Grandfather's caution saves the day, and so on. The opposite adjustment can create more cynical outcomes: villainy saves the day, Grandfather's caution leads to punishment. Or they can choose to shut the machine down altogether, at least for a moment, diconnecting cause from effect to offer readers a glimpse into a truly random world, with all of the horror or comedy that might contain.

Whether they make such large adjustments as these, or just indulge in gentle fettling, writers need a good working knowledge of the Machinery of Consequences, along with an old rag and a pocketful of well-oiled tools.

The machinery plays a part in many of the stories in this volume. Watch, for example, as events drag the protagonist of Robert Summersgill's 'The Menagerie of Sound' towards the story's conclusion, or the way that a relationship falters on the same ideas on which it was founded in S R Mastrantone's 'Something Unfinished'.

Tony Lovell's 'The Stairwell' follows on from a fleeting friendship during the childhood of its protagonist, while in 'The System', from Warwick Sprawson, the consequences will take place after the story, and they'll probably be none too pleasant. In Ian Shine's 'Love Stops at Ten Metres', a conversation that's intended to be a consequence in itself instead has consequences of its own, while our new story from Ian Sales might result from events that reach back to the very beginning of the last century.

The consequences of war or economic upheaval play their parts in new stories from Matt Plass, Paul Lenehan, and Tania Hershman, and... you get the idea. Throughout these stories, the Machinery of Consequences operates in the background, while the writer oils a cog, changes a gear, or disconnects a cable altogether for a moment or two.

Six of the stories in *Because of What Happened* are shorter than usual: these are the winning and shortlisted entries from our new annual flash fiction competition. The first prize went to Tania Hershman for 'A Call to Arms', but it could have gone to any, or all, of the shortlisted stories: each in its own way makes wonderful use of the limited space available, and taken together they demonstrate the variety and scope that can be achieved with very short fiction.

'Invisible Them' is Matt's third appearance in our anthology series. See also his story 'Tripe Soup and Spanish Wine' in Crying Just Like Anybody, *and the title story in* The Maginot Line, *for which he won the Fiction Desk Writer's Award.*

Invisible Them

Matt Plass

The photograph, Jacob fresh in uniform, stands on the television and sometimes David tests her, asks what just happened in the programme they watch together. When she can't answer he knows where her eyes have been.

Jacob's coat, heavy with its fur hood, hangs on its peg in the hall. He may need it when he's home. Yes, it's July but who wants the trouble of going up in the loft twice?

They don't watch the news: they watch the phone. Annie with her brown rabbit's eyes, David with the back of his neck. David says, 'What's the use worrying about something that won't happen?'

He reads. *How can he do that?* she thinks.

In the first days they argued about setting the table for three. She laughed, kept it light, silently begged David to let it go. No, he wouldn't. 'We aren't in mourning, this doesn't define us. There'll be opportunity enough to set three places at Christmas.'

Friday evenings, Jacob calls, when he can. When he can't, no one sleeps and Saturday is a fug. The best Fridays are when Jacob calls early and they wave at each other through the tiny square of Skype window. Jacob's chatter outruns the frames-per-second, words tumbling from the speakers. Annie expands the window; never mind the pixellation, here's a face you could hold in your hands. An early evening call, however brief, purchases minutes, hours, of peace in the small, quiet spaces of their home.

September. The calls come less often, Jacob misses two Fridays in a row. David tells Annie to go to her doctor, get him to give her something, but she won't.

When Jacob does call, his voice is slower, heavy. He won't talk about his work, but fires questions that loop like dud missiles to fall into the ocean between them. How are they? How is Mr Hooper's dog? What's the weather, good as last year?

'He's adjusting,' says David. 'Same as when he tried university. A call a day, then one a week, then we had to call him just to know he was alive.'

That word isn't allowed in the house, Annie thinks, licking a drop of salt water from her lip. If you let that word in, you have to allow its brother in too.

But they are proud, so proud. Folk ask after Jacob, at the corner shop, in The Crown. David and Annie feel the tang and puff of celebrity. Why shouldn't they? They are contributing, too. By carrying on. Keeping their chins up.

David catches himself dwelling on the manner he'll adopt if it happens. How he'll do grief. He is ashamed of the thoughts and doesn't share them with Annie.

Throughout October, Jacob fails to call. One day, when David is out, Annie breaks. She telephones the barracks in Chester. A voice promises to check and puts Annie on hold for twenty minutes, no music, a deep well of silence. Then the voice is back. 'No,' it says, 'Jacob is alive; sometimes the comms go down; it happens.' The voice offers to get a message to Jacob.

The family Skype in early November. Jacob is in shadow, sat back from the screen. He talks about 'invisible them'. He says, 'We need to send a message.' He says something about mascara but the line distorts.

David says, 'Hang in there.' Annie asks if he's okay. Jacob laughs and it's not a nice sound.

David and Annie don't watch the news so they don't see the newsflash, the sombre anchorwoman. Cut to a young man in British military gear, his head covered, bundled into a dusty car by military police. Cut to a squat dun hut, coy footage of sandalled child's legs at an unnatural angle. Cut to women head to toe in black, making that sound they make out there. Cut to a mad-blind crowd burning flags in a dusty street.

They don't hear the studio speculation, or the words *rogue, civilian casualties, murder,* or *disgrace.* They miss the expert's comments about the impact of trauma on the psyche of serving personnel.

Now, David and Annie wash up together. Annie is first to see the car turn into their drive. Two suits get out. Not suits: uniforms now the caps are on.

Annie dries her hands and wonders why they didn't send a woman. They always send a woman in the movies. It's David not Annie who sinks to his knees in the doorway, even before a word is spoken.

'It's not what you think,' says the taller uniform and Annie's heart vaults. She has prepared for the worst. Anything else will be a blessing.

Coventry-based journalist Cindy George is making her Fiction Desk debut with this new story.

The Coaster Boys

Cindy George

The first couple of times you go on a ride, your organs feel like they're being thrown around your body, and the only reason you're not being sick is you don't know where your stomach is. After the first few times, you seem to get a kind of physical memory: something in your blood knows where the lifts and the drops and the inversions are, and you start to lean into it. I've been on Nemesis seventy-eight times; Jas has done about sixty. Some of the other lads have done hundreds. We got into it at school. It was Bungee Farren's birthday, we were all fourteen, and his parents, braver than I would have been, took six of us to Alton Towers. Ryan and Jack came with us again a couple of times, but lost interest once they got girlfriends and guitars. Me and Jas and Bungee and Neil, though, we couldn't get enough. It was our thing.

We started calling ourselves the Coaster Boys; yeah, I know how shit that sounds. Even when we were fourteen we knew it sounded shit, and bear in mind we thought Craig David and the after-school chess club were cool. For the next two or three years, there was loads of pestering various parents to drive up and down motorways, and we started to meet other people as well: you'd start to see the same faces at the opening of a new ride, or the preview days you'd sometimes get invited to before the parks opened for the season. They told us about the forums for ride enthusiasts, and we met even more people online. I suppose I could say I've made twenty or thirty good friends from theme parking. The four of us, though, have always stuck together, we're the core, and me and Jas, we're the core de la core. If that's a thing.

It didn't take long for us to get into the whole culture of the parks. We're on friendly terms with most of the workers on the maintenance and engineering sides: we call them Oompa Loompas, they call us geeks, it's fair. We can hold our own in a conversation about different types and makes of rides. We know the differences between a Gerstlauer construction and an Intamin, and which one's better and why. None of us ended up becoming ride engineers, but we have all got jobs; well, Jas hasn't now, of course. Bungee's a lawyer, if you can believe it. Hope I never get arrested, just because I don't want to ever have to find out whether he's any good or not. Bungee and Neil got married, not to each other. I'm single at the moment, and I'm not totally sure, but I think Jas might be about to die a virgin. We were always talking about girls of course, but he never went out with anyone for more than a few weeks, and I don't remember him ever saying anything about sex that sounded authentic. It's definite now that he's going to die. He's probably only got a few weeks, but he says he's going to try and make it to his twenty-fifth, just so we've got to waste money on presents for him. He looks bloody horrible, so if he hasn't had sex by now, it's not a great time to start.

Jas somehow managed to get breast cancer. Stupid tit. Yes, we're still doing that joke; it's irresistible. None of us even knew blokes could get it, till he got it. That's part of why it got so bad actually, he had problems for months before he saw a doctor, it just hadn't occurred to him it could be anything like that. It is ridiculously rare, which is why he's even more of a twat for getting it.

The day after he got told, we went to Alton Towers. We call it our home park: it was our first, and it's still the nearest for us all to get together, even though Bungee and Neil moved up to Manchester for uni and never left.

'You'd better get some extra time in on Nemmy and Blivvy, just in case it's your last time, sicklad,' said Bungee as we rolled into the car park, and Jas poked him in the ribs, making him squeal like a girl. (Yes, we do have pet names for our favourite rides. We wouldn't go around calling them 'Nemesis' and 'Oblivion' just like normal people, would we?) We'd had the trip planned for weeks, we weren't trying to cheer ourselves up or anything. In fact we'd brought a couple of Bungee's most boring old law college books with us for the photos, the ones they take at the point in the ride when you're supposed to be screaming with your hands in the air. They show everyone's photos at the exit shop, so we always like to pretend to be reading books or playing cards or asleep or something in ours. We never buy them, but it gives everyone a laugh when they come off the ride. Jas wanted to pretend to be having a heart attack but we wouldn't let him in case he got us barred.

We've been to Orlando and Miami, the four of us, just to go on rides, and we've been on some of the best there are, and eaten Florida portions of burger and fries afterwards and never been sick. We've been to all the biggest and best parks in the UK, and some of the smallest and worst, and it's always, always been brilliant. Nothing's like the Towers, though. Once you've come off the A52 and you catch that first glimpse in the distance, there's always a big cheer in the car, and usually some unnecessary male bonding behaviour. It feels like the moment between waking up on Christmas morning when you're six, and actually seeing your presents.

Over lunch that day at the Towers, Jas announced: 'If I ever go into a coma or anything, I don't want my favourite pop stars hanging around at my bedside.' We looked at him. 'Firstly, it'd be embarrassing,' he expanded. 'I'd be in my pyjamas and everything. Also, the pop stars I like are all mental. No one wants to see a bloke with maracas and a mad hat coming through a hospital ward towards them. If I wake up and there's someone like that there, I'm going to pretend I'm still in the coma. So for Rog's sake just promise me that one thing.' We decided in sixth form that God's name must be Roger. None of us can now remember why, but it seems as likely as anything, so that's what we call him.

We've stopped talking about it now so much, though. When Jas first got ill, when we all thought he was going to get better, we used to spend hours planning his funeral. We haven't said anything like that for ages. If he doesn't still want Kylie played, he'd better say so soon, because that's the last instruction I had. Now he keeps talking about, 'oh, when I get better', even though it was him who told us in the first place he wasn't going to get better.

There's this weird and horrible sort of glamour attached to waiting for your best friend to die. Katie came up to me and Bungee in the pub one night and started saying to me, 'It's so great that you're doing things for Jas, looking after him and everything. I really admire you, you know.' It made me feel a bit sick and uneasy. It's not as if I'm round his house every day wiping his arse for him. I just haven't stopped being me, and he hasn't stopped being him, and we're mates; that's all. I'm not doing anything for him, just being normal. It put me off Katie a bit, to be honest, and then I felt guilty for that, she hadn't meant anything by it.

And in any case, I haven't seen as much of him lately. Well, he's been in and out of hospital, and he can't get out as much. But also, I find myself just accidentally not going to see him sometimes. Sometimes I'd rather talk to the others. Just because it's not long now before I won't have him to talk to, and I don't want to be left completely on my own. I was thinking about going round to see him the other day, but I knew he'd be all groggy because of whatever drugs he's on at the moment, and I ended up chatting on American coaster forums all night instead. I sent him a funny email to make up for it, but I don't know if he's reading them these days. His mum reads him his messages sometimes when his eyes are funny, so I always start off with a 'hello' to her, just to remind me not to say anything inappropriate. Not that I think anything would shock her – I mean, she knows him better than I do. It must be hard for her though to read our daft messages, or when I barrel into their house all healthy and cheerful with all my plans for the future and news of things we've done without him. She surprised me one day last week by standing on the doorstep as I was leaving and saying 'Rob' – she normally only ever calls me Robert – 'would you mind… will you still come and see us sometimes afterwards?' I said 'of course' without even thinking about it, just because right at that moment I would have agreed to do whatever she wanted. I thought it was a bit weird, though. 'I thought you'd be sick of seeing me by now, Mrs S.,' I said, wondering if she would say why she would want to inherit me as a friend from her son. But she just smiled and then Jas's sister was coming up the path, so it was all just waves and smiles and 'hi, bye' and all that till I got out of the gate.

I got a text from Jas later that night saying, 'u left yr book u idiot & btw mum wants to adopt u.' I sent one back saying, 'I thought you had cancer, not dyslexia. Will pick up book tomorrow.' Then I thought about it a bit and sent another one saying, 'we will take your mum to the Towers for a day out soon.' I meant after he'd died. To be honest I was half thinking we might scatter some of his ashes there. The message I got back from him read 'ok but NO SWEARING & DO NOT let her go on Blivvy or eat the hot dogs.' It was nice to think of us connected by these silly messages, both smiling at the same thing on different sides of town.

I had this stupid dream that night. I dreamed that the most amazing new dark coaster had been built in Las Vegas of all places, Rog knows why there. And me and Jas – who was healthy and normal in the dream – were waiting to go on it. But when we got to the front of the queue, the guy stopped me. Jas got on, but they wouldn't let me on with him, and I was going mad, because we'd come all that way, but Jas went off on this ride, all excited, and I was so disappointed. As his car started the ascent, he was laughing at me, really pissing himself, with that stupid guffaw of his, and waving sarcastically, then he wasn't there anymore. When I woke up, I was crying, and one side of my face was stuck to the pillow with snot. I thought at first I might have been sick or something, then I just felt stupid, and a bit disgusted with myself. But I rang Neil as soon as I was properly awake to tell him about it, and about taking Jas's mum with us next time, and since then, I've felt more like going to a park than I had done for ages.

S R Mastrantone won the Fiction Desk Writer's Award for his story in Crying Just Like Anybody.

Something Unfinished

S R Mastrantone

October 14th

Dear Eric,

I hope this finds you and Julia well. I assume that Rebecca has taken to big school like the proverbial duck? What about Richard? His turn next. Is he nervous yet? Send them Grandad's love.

I'll try and answer the questions posed in your email, but let me begin by reassuring you that your mother and I are both safe and with friends in warmer climes. I have no doubt that with the great minds at your disposal in life and at the university you could probably use that information alone to deduce our separate whereabouts, but I warn you that it really won't help matters and would be a waste of your time and money. Both of us will return to England at some point in the future once we have wrapped our minds around what has happened.

Your confusion is understandable. I am not so ancient that I can't appreciate that our decision to divorce is unusual. I do resent the slightly ageist overtones in your email, but given you must be in shock I am willing to overlook that. Perhaps you will feel slightly more understanding once I have explained.

It happened on the last day of August. A normal enough day to begin with. We woke up late; I made a pot of tea and some eggs on toast and then took Puzzle for a walk. I came back, your mother and I had a friendly disagreement about that Libyan terrorist the government freed and then sometime late in the afternoon I took Puzzle out again. It was raining and I got drenched. On my return I had a hot bath then joined your mother in the lounge.

For ten minutes we watched the news in silence; nothing extraordinary about that, of course. But another ten minutes after that I thought it slightly odd that neither of us had commented on the Libyan terrorist piece. I opened my mouth to mention this but found I couldn't speak. My jaw hung open in anticipation of words but despite my greatest effort, no words came. Eventually I had to force it closed again, my attempt to talk abandoned. I must have looked like a goldfish.

Your mother looked over at me, inquisitive and amused. She opened her own mouth, but nothing came out. Her face did the same fish impression I imagine my own face had made.

I tried to speak again, to apologise (force of habit), but once more there was nothing there to say. Nothing there. It reminded me of attempting a sprint at the final section of the 3000 metre race in my school days, trying my best to please those well-meaning but sadistic onlookers shouting encouragements but finding that all I had the energy left to do was pull my best exertion face.

For the longest time we sat looking at each other. Occasionally one of us would try again.

Flap. Flap. Flap. Get your fresh fish here!

I stood up and went into the kitchen and made a cup of tea. 'Oh dear,' I said. The words were effortless. 'Oh dear, dear me.'

I took your mother her tea. Her eyes were shimmering. I smiled at her, trying to send a message with my eyes: *Ivy, we knew this would happen*. I don't know if it helped her, but when I went upstairs and packed my bags, saying it out loud to the empty room made me feel better.

When we said goodbye in the porch your mother's eyes were dry. We shook hands. We both nodded. As I left I turned back, the romantic in me always the last to accept reality. The door was closing. I went to say something but only when the door shut was I able to eject the words. If anyone had been watching they would have seen an old man shouting, '– you always,' at an empty drive.

I drove back to Blythe to stay with your uncle. He was suitably appalled and suggested I might be mentally ill. He phoned your mother. From the lounge I could just about hear her voice on the other end of the phone: tinny, tiny, and incomprehensible. It made me wonder about the parameters of our plight. Even though we couldn't talk to each other any more, what would happen if the speaker phone was on? Could I just listen to her? And if one-sided communication was permissible, what if I tried writing to her? Would a similar palsy as had stricken my tongue prevent me putting pen to paper?

On considering these things I decided it didn't really matter if it were possible or not. In the end what we were experiencing were symptoms of a terminal condition. Of course you might find ways to circumvent the thing, buy yourself another day or two. But what is the point?

Sorry, perhaps I am jumping ahead here.

When Gerry had finished talking to your mother it was another few moments before he joined me. He handed me a tumbler of whisky and took a long sip from his own. 'Harry, I think you and Ivy both need committing.'

I frowned but inside I was buoyed that your mother didn't seem be having any difficulty accepting what was happening.

Your uncle has never been one for using his brain, but that isn't to say he is stupid: by the end of the night I am convinced he understood. I confess I garbled some of it and at times had to over-simplify. So while he grasped the salient points I knew that when the time came to explain it to you, I would have to do better.

You've heard the story a hundred times from your mother: Cambridge, 1955, leaves brown and brittle; she cycles across Magdalene bridge, then falls off her bike, only to be helped back to her feet by a handsome young man who whisks her off for a cheer-up cup of tea. I've always preferred her version and have often found myself reporting it to people as if it were what actually happened.

It isn't relevant, but what really occurred was I crossed the road without looking and she careered into me. If the thought that I was handsome crossed her mind at all, it can't have been until later: she was livid, inviting her for a cup of tea was the only thing I could do to stop her castigating my clumsiness.

We went to a nearby pub. I left your mother muttering curses by an open fire. When I returned she was frowning and looking intently at her watch.

'I am terribly sorry,' I said and set the tea down in front of her. 'They say we philosophers always have our heads in the clouds. That's probably why I ran straight into you.' I laughed, she didn't.

'You're one of those, are you?' She gave a quick flick of her eyebrows.

'You don't like philosophy?' I asked.

'I wouldn't say that. But I'm not terribly impressed by this Mr Ayer and his acolytes. Surely turning philosophy in on language itself sort of spoils the fun?'

'I tend to agree. I prefer the classics. Plato, Aristo–'

'Ah, the theory of the forms. So lovely.'

I sipped my tea. 'He was a bit of a despot though, no?'

'Plato?'

'Yes. Didn't a certain German leader think himself quite the philosopher king? Seeing the shadows on the wall for what they really were?'

Her frown intensified. 'I think you're reading Plato as if he were Mr Ayer. Plato was a Greek and I think deserving of a more sympathetic reading.'

I thought she studied philosophy too, but was in a different year, perhaps. 'What do you read?' I asked.

'History.'

'How do you know Ayer and Plato then?'

'My school invented a subject called Intellectual Tools. We did logic puzzles and talked about philosophy.' She looked into the fire and I thought I could see a trace of a smile.

'Where did you go to school?'

'St. Margaret's.'

'Not in Birmingham?'

'Marlstone, actually. But yes. Do you know it?'

I smiled and leaned forward. 'I went to St. Peters. You're from the Midlands too?'

'Well, our family's from North Wales but we moved there when I was ten.'

'Where in North Wales? My grandmother has a log cabin there. Near Trawsfyndd?'

She grinned and her eyes grew wide. 'Nearby actually. Capel Celyn. Between Bala and Traws.'

'I know it, isn't that in the valley they want to flood to make a reservoir?'

Her grin retreated. 'You don't think they'll actually approve such a plan do you? The chapel alone is hundreds of years old.'

'That didn't stop them flooding Lake Vyrnwy.'

'How do you know about these places?'

'My grandmother has us well drilled. She likes us to impress the locals when we stay. And I find Wales intriguing. It's a colony really, isn't it?'

Your mother leaned forward and picked up her satchel. She reached inside and pulled out a pad and paper and looked up at me, the tentative smile back on her lips. 'You're starting to unsettle me a little bit,' she said and handed the pad over. Scrawled on the page were notes for an essay, the title of which was underlined at the top of the page: *Wales: The First Colony.*

Two hours later I walked your mother to the porter's lodge at St. John's. After our intense conversations, all we had left were nervous smiles and clumsy eye contact. We shook hands and then your mother leaned forward and kissed me full on the lips. 'Thank you,' I said and she laughed.

We left one another that night feeling as if there was something unfinished between us.

On my way home I became amused at how important this hitherto unknown woman now felt. Memories of my life just three hours previous filled me with sorrow. How had I ever found the enthusiasm for anything before her?

I was in love, of course. But the philosopher in me was not satisfied with that. Love? The concept needed unpacking. What were its necessary and sufficient conditions? When was love truly love? How could we verify that?

It would take a long time before I pieced the puzzle together, but that night I kept returning to one word: unfinished.

On the one-year anniversary of our fortuitous collision, we went to my grandmother's cabin for the weekend. We went to a local inn and found a roaring fire. After a pint of the local beer, we reminisced about that first encounter.

'Do you remember what we talked about?' your mother asked.

'Some of it,' I replied. 'We put the entire world to rights?'

'Didn't we just. We couldn't finish one conversation because we'd already be on to the next.'

'It is funny how that happens, isn't it? When you really connect with someone. We kept bouncing from one thing to another... We never concluded a single discussion.'

'Do conversations need concluding?'

'I don't know? We never did get to the bottom of Ayer versus Plato.' She laughed. 'But you know, I remember leaving you that night feeling unsatisfied. But looking back perhaps it was because all those little conversations were...'

'...unfinished,' your mother said, her eyes focussed not on me, but at some point between me and the flames.

'Yes.'

For a while we were silent. Then she said: 'It would be funny if our whole relationship, I mean if all relationships were the consequence of unfinished conversations.'

I laughed. 'Yes,' I said. It was an idea that had been lodged at the tip of my tongue since the night we had met.

'No need to be so excited about it.'

'I had it the night we met. I kept thinking about how it felt like we still had things to talk about. Things to settle. That even though we had been talking for hours, it felt like we were just starting. Do you think that is, perhaps, what love is?' Your mother shrugged, a mischievous twinkle in her eye.

We retired early that evening, giddy with beer and belief. It felt as if we had uncovered some tremendous truth.

It took me until the next morning, always where I find my darkest thoughts, to fully realise what it all meant. Your mother was still asleep and I went for a walk around the lake. There it hit me, the question we were too drunk to ask: What if during the course of a relationship, all those unfinished conversations resolve? Instantly I thought of my own parents, sitting at the dinner table every night in silence. I thought of those older couples that would always frown at your mother and I when we ate in restaurants; when we talked loudly and passionately. Those couples that couldn't even look at each other anymore.

I ran back to the cabin and woke your mother. She tried her best to calm me, stroked my arm and made me breakfast. 'But throughout a lifetime with someone you continually start new conversations that go unresolved,' she said. But she didn't sound convinced.

·

After that, we were always aware of it. It hung over us.

We were scared of talking about things that reminded us of that first. We were scared of concluding those conversations.

We tried our best not to talk about Plato, Ayer, Cambridge, Hitler... But you can never really be sure what it is you are really talking about in a relationship, can you?

Once, just after you were born, we did talk about Ayer. It was an argument. We didn't argue much, as you know, but this one was a bloodbath. Your mother only mentioned Ayer because she was angry and said that there was no point trying to 'eschew the inevitable.' When we made up, we held each other and agreed that should it ever happen, should we ever just find that we no longer had words for one another, we would end it. We wouldn't drag our dead love to the restaurant to glare at younger lovers still caught in their own discussions; we wouldn't die side-by-side but miserable. With tears in our eyes we mourned our parting in advance of the event. But in doing so, we knew that if our time came, it would be swift and painless.

Do you understand now?

It did not occur to me until I reached your uncle's house in August, but the final piece was the argument your mother and I had about the Libyan terrorist. I thought it was awful they had freed him. The people on that plane not only died, but they were more than likely alive for the two terrifying minutes it took the plane to fall to the ground. What compassion does the perpetrator of such an act deserve?

'What if he didn't do it?' your mother said.

'The point is the law deems he did do it but is still deserving of compassion.'

'But isn't the point that they might have got it wrong?'

'If that's the case he should be freed, not released on compassionate grounds. The law is the law.'

Your mother smiled as if she had just forced a checkmate. She couldn't have had any idea what she was about to do. 'But that's like the problem of the philosopher king, isn't it? Your issue with Plato is that no man could ever know what is truly good, the *form* of the good. Thus the law can't be black and white because we mortals can never access the truth. Isn't that why you oppose the death penalty too? The law should always err on the side of caution.'

She had a good point. In noble defeat I had risen and taken out the dog to mull over my mistake. I wonder if I could have spoken to her then or whether the process takes a while to set in once that final conversation resolves? An academic point, I suppose.

I have done my best to explain. I accept that you will be reluctant to accept what I have told you, partly due to what it might make you feel about your own marriage. But as always, please do not attack the man just because you dislike the argument. For what it is worth I don't think that every relationship always gets the chance to run its course. Some are lucky enough to never reach that final point. All I ask is that you accept that your mother and I did reach that point, and that we have acted in a manner fitting of the love we had for each other.

I will be in touch again when I head home. When that will be is still a mystery even to me, but I look forward to dinner and a fine wine when that time comes.

Best for now,

Dad (MA Cantab)

December 1st

Dad,

I am glad you're well and warm. It's taken me some time to get my own head around what you wrote to us, and even more time to put it in some words that the kids might understand. Unsurprisingly, they are baffled. I admit this is probably my fault for not really understanding it in the first place, but I blame the lucid but crazed source material.

We are doing a good impression of understanding it to anyone that asks. It mostly involves explaining the situation while pulling a face that conveys we think you both might have lost your minds.

The other day I told Rebecca and Richard I was struggling to think of what to write to you. I asked if they had anything to say. They both shook their heads. I jokingly said: 'If you say nothing, Granddad will think you don't love him.'

To which Rebecca said: 'I love Richard but sometimes I just don't want to talk to him.'

That is where we are at the moment, Dad. We all love you very much, but at the moment we don't really have the words.

I hope you don't take it personally.

Love,

Eric

We see a lot of fiction written in the second person, and often there's no reason for it; it can be fatiguing, like watching a film entirely shot with a SnorriCam. Sometimes, though, it's just right, as is the case with this story from Paul Lenehan.

For Joy

Paul Lenehan

No, but you have to stay positive. You buy your house during the boom and the day after you move in the banks crash, the euro slumps to an all-time low, and they open a methadone clinic just six doors down from your des res, addicts on the pavement at all hours discussing the global crisis in a manner best described as agitated. No problem, you were keen to live in an area noted for its local colour, and here you are. Happy days. Then you discover your next-door neighbour's a persistent drink-driving mother with a husband due out of prison after serving time for GBH. Big deal, you're a fan of the grittier TV soaps, now you're living in one. It'll be a laugh.

And you're a dog lover, so you count yourself blessed that the view from your front window takes in a patch of waste ground where hooded youths at twilight lead pit bull terriers for their nightly frolics. And so what if your modest budget has meant a move to this rural town only intermittently visited by Irish Rail? No problem, you can rumble to work on a bus by the scenic route. And if the fifty miles from your office is extended to twice that distance because the bus diverts to pick up every religious outing and pensioners' day trip in every parish in a ten-mile radius of the highway, well, that'll liven up the journey no end. Okay so, who's going to start the sing-song?

You've got to stay upbeat, even when www.deathclock.com – which uses your age and the standard life expectancy tables as data – reveals that your forty-year mortgage is due to terminate on the same day on which you can expect to die. Sure all you'll need is a little luck and you'll legally own your semi-detached before rigor mortis has quite set in. That, you tell yourself, is something to look forward to.

Then it's the first weekend in your new home and you listen to the al fresco methadone clinic choir give a raucous interpretation of 'Hit Me Baby One More Time', the pre-meltdown Britney Spears anthem. From far away you hear a jangling noise, like a huge spillage of cutlery: that'll be the bottom, you note wryly, falling out of the market. But best to stay on-message. So you begin to count your blessings.

Health is number one, sanity number two, also in the top ten is the amicable relationship you still enjoy with your ex-wife, now living in Dingle / An Daingean with her dietician. You count up to sixty-seven (your rotary mower with its 1700 watt hi-torque motor), or even as far as seventy-six (your favourite line of poetry, *A bracelet of bright hair about the bone*), before your tired eyes begin to close. And it's inevitable, with over 14,600 such evenings still to come, that you begin to sob. But there's no use in moping. You're weeping for joy, you tell yourself; this is for joy.

Tim Lay is the author of a novel, The Sewerside Chronicles, *and* NIBS, *a book of short stories. This is his first Fiction Desk appearance.*

The Patter of Tiny Feet

Tim Lay

His hands were always oily. That's what I remember about Cal. Even when they were clean the grooves that ran across his palms and fingers were ingrained with black. I'm not sure that he was even a mechanic by trade. He just liked messing around with engines.

Was he one of my mother's boyfriends? Too many years have gone by that I would even want to ask. Neither can I remember how long he lived at the farm. Back then there were always people who came to stay and didn't leave.

We called it a farm, but this was somewhat of an exaggeration. It was more of a small holding: a labourer's cottage, a half converted barn, some outbuildings and five acres of land on the edge of Exmoor. My mother had turned twenty-one and used a small trust fund to buy her way into a fantasy of hippy self-sufficiency without paying much thought to the practicalities. A lot of the time, life on the farm was harsh and our years there throb in my memory as the very best of summer and the very worst of winter.

Unlike the others, Cal wore his hair short, in a crew cut, maybe because he didn't want to get it covered in oil. I only ever remember him wearing a boiler suit. Not a regular boiler suit, but something tan, moleskin, with a German flag on the sleeve.

Cal wasn't very forthcoming. He wasn't cold or unkind, just carried himself with an air of indifference. He never made an effort to befriend us kids and for this reason the others tended to avoid him. Strangely though, I was drawn to his ambivalence. I suspect that, even aged six, I had already developed a dislike for hippies and their communal dreams and pious platitudes.

One of the outbuildings was known as the workshop and it was here that Cal spent much of his time. I would hang at the door, watching him as he took oily things apart and put them back together again. I asked a lot of questions and he rarely answered me. Over time however I asked fewer questions and he began to tell me more.

Most who passed through the farm had travelled. I knew Marrakech, Delhi, Kabul almost as well as if I'd been there myself through the many stories I'd heard from those drifting back from the trail. But Cal's stories were different. He'd seen the world working ships and his tales came from Zanzibar, Manila, Penang, and seas that teemed with pirates and man-eating sharks.

We were in the workshop. The engine of someone's van lay in pieces on the floor and I'd made a game of tiptoeing between them, until Cal told me to stop.

'What's in there?' I asked and pointed to a barrel that had recently 'arrived'. It was taller than I was and stood in a corner.

Cal looked up from what he was doing. 'Nothing,' he replied and went back to the oily lump of metal on the worktop.

'What's it for, then?'

'Rats,' he said, after a while. Cal always took a while to reply.

'Are they going to live in it?' I asked.

My six-year-old logic saw Cal, perhaps through the act of blowing a tune on a pipe, calling up all the rats to take up a new home in the barrel.

Cal didn't say anything.

On the farm, our world revolved around the kitchen. For one, it was the cosiest place to be with its Rayburn and the fire that burnt away through the winter, but it was also the place where the farm dwellers came to share food and company; jamming and laughing, or debating long into the night on everything from what seeds should be planted where, to which part of the world revolution should be planted next. On the farm, everyone had their say and decisions were rarely taken lightly.

I remember that spring, when the only tune on the radio seemed to be 'Tiger Feet' by Mud, the topic of conversation was often the rats. We were seeing quite a few of them by then. To begin with, some thought it was a good thing. One resident in particular, a man called Bob with hair so long he could sit on it, regularly invoked the example of a temple in India where thousands of rats were worshipped. However, by the time the daffodils were pushing through, the rats had become a problem that could no longer be denied. They were no longer an occasional sighting in the chicken coop at dusk, or a scuttling sound in the outbuildings. Food bins got savaged, walls got chewed, cables got gnawed and that scuttling sound was regularly under my bed at night.

One morning I opened the larder door and encountered a particularly large rat that eyed me contemptuously from one of the shelves inside.

At some point, around the kitchen table, it was agreed that Mother Nature was not going to intervene to restore the natural equilibrium. But of course we lived in a Shangri-La of hippy ideals. We didn't do poison on the farm. We laid traps. They were home-made and humane and remained unsprung. We got another cat. It disappeared. The discussions continued until the day that Cal stood up and said, 'I'll deal with it.' I can't remember the conversation that preceded this comment, but I do remember, quite vividly, the rift that seemed to divide the room once he'd left.

Cal wasn't around when I pushed open the door to the workshop. I was about to close it when I noticed that a large board, weighted down with stones, now lay over the top of the barrel. I came towards it for a better look and that's when I heard a noise, a light thud from inside. I reached out to touch the side of the barrel.

'What are you doing?'

The sharpness of Cal's tone made me jump. He stood in the doorway, glaring at me.

I didn't apologise or cry or go running to my mother. I was a hippy kid, remember.

I asked questions.

'What's in there?'

'Rats,' he replied. He knocked the mud off his boots and closed the door behind him.

'How many?'

He shrugged. 'A few.'

'Where did they come from?'

Cal huffed. He scratched his head. 'I just came in this morning and they were there,' he said at last. He walked over to the barrel and pressed a palm against the board to check it was in place.

'What are you going to do with them?'

Cal wavered. I've told you before that he took his time, and now he seemed to take double even that. 'Nothing,' he said slowly.

'Can I see?'

He shook his head. 'I want you to promise me something.' He moved forward and then, as if I had a force field around me, he stopped. 'I want you to promise you won't ever try to take the lid off.'

I nodded sincerely. 'Why?'

Almost as soon as the question left my lips there came a high pitched squeal that rose up from deep inside the barrel, piercing my ears and spreading alarm through my body. If you've ever heard the squeal of a cornered rat you'll know why. It can haunt your dreams forever. I moved towards Cal, right through that force field, until I stood looking up at him. He reached out a hand, and hesitated before laying it lightly on my shoulder. 'Come on,' he said. 'I think it's best you stay out of the workshop for a while.'

Staying out of the workshop became a rule in the house with no rules, and the workshop door became locked in a house without locks. This released a strange atmosphere into the farm. Nothing was ever said in front of us kids – and at that time there were a few – but something had split our kitchen table community along invisible lines.

Looking back, I now realise that Cal was never really liked by anyone apart from my mother. He was practical, fixed people's buses, made the barn a better place to stay.

For this the others tolerated him. But he wasn't the same as them and for this I think they always distrusted him. In the days that followed I heard things – mumbled comments and random mutterings about a Dr Mengele and his workshop. Of course, I assumed they were talking about a new arrival on the farm.

On the topic of the barrel in the workshop, the grown-ups in the house of no lies told us the rats were being tamed so they wouldn't bother us anymore. We were young enough that it was explanation enough, but that locked door was taken by us a sign that something really special must be happening in there. Just to stand with your ear at the heavy oak door provoked a sense of excitement I'd never felt before. I imagined Cal on the other side of it in a ringmaster's top hat and tails, taming his six rats.

As the days went past I wondered if he'd let me have one.

I'd already thought of a name.

It was Cal who jumped when he heard me scuffing my feet at the doorway. He was standing over the barrel. The lid was off and he was peering inside. His head snapped in my direction.

'Hey,' he said. 'You're not supposed to be in here.'

'Let me see,' I pleaded.

He thought too long about his reply and by that time I was already there, hands outstretched towards the lip of the barrel. Instinctively, Cal slapped them away. Not used to being smacked I recoiled. He must've felt bad because he told me he was sorry.

'You just need to be careful where you're putting your fingers,' he told me.

'Can I see?' I asked, clasping my stinging hands behind my back.

'There's not much to see.'

'Please.'

He tutted and stooped to pick me up, leaning me forward just enough that I could see inside. The sides of the barrel were mottled stages of rusty decay – orange, black, red, brown – that blended into the darkness of the bottom. At first I saw nothing, and then a movement drew my eyes, peeling back the bad light so that I could make out the shape of the rat sitting in the base of the barrel. It was so large I thought at first it was a cat. It sat on its thick brown tail, propped up on its haunches as it groomed its shiny fur, so dark it was almost black. After a moment it stopped. It cocked its head purposefully and in our direction and looked right into my eyes. Instinctively I leaned back into Cal.

'Is he tame?' I whispered.

'Getting there,' he said softly.

The rat went back to its grooming.

I suddenly realised. 'Where are the others?'

Cal sighed. 'Gone,' he said at last.

He put me down and replaced the lid on the barrel.

'You have to go now, he said.

'Can we call him Achilles?' I asked.

Cal laughed, a murmuring laugh that came from his throat. 'I think we probably can.'

It's funny how things become clear over time. Those moments when memories are suddenly seen for what they actually were instead of what they seemed to be at the time.

The penny dropped for me, after thirty-five years, in an air-conditioned bar at the Traders Hotel in Penang. I sell agrochemicals, and I was with a client who worked in the rice business. Yeah, I know: so much for the hippy upbringing. I tell my mother I do work for the UN. He began to tell me a story. I think it had become an anecdote he told to westerners to pick him out as modern and forward thinking.

Deep in rural Indonesia, he told me, rats plague the paddy fields, probably because snakes, their biggest natural predator, aren't allowed to thrive. Many small farmers either can't afford modern poisons or distrust them, so have their own method of controlling the rat population. A farmer will catch several rats and place them in a bucket with no food and little water.

A number of days later, only one rat will be left. One more rat will be added and the two are left in the bucket until only one rat remains again. This remaining rat is now a cannibal rat. To survive, it has feasted on many rats, and now it has the taste for the flesh of its own kind. It is said that once the cannibal rat is released, that rat will enter a colony and scare the others away.

My client finished the story. 'I suppose you could call it organic pest control,' he said and cracked a laugh, which I returned. It would've been impolite not to. He shook his head. 'These are the kind of guys we are up against. They must catch up to the modern world.'

The contracts signed, we moved to the restaurant and I ate a steak the size of my arm while we talked agrochemicals. After dinner I returned to my hotel room. To the hum of the air con, I slipped beneath the down duvet and lay there, looking up at the ceiling, thinking about Cal and the rats on the farm.

Robert Summersgill, a recent graduate from the Creative Writing course at Bath Spa, is making his fiction debut with the following story.

The Menagerie of Sound

Robert Summersgill

I wake at 7:44 exactly. There is no middle ground, just a jump from unconsciousness to full alertness. I lie still, savouring the silence. Counting the seconds off with my fingers. Three, two, one... A klaxon begins to screech. It is the sort of sound that bites the inside of your ears.

7:45. Time to get up. I roll off my bedding and take a step into the middle of the room. Turn left. Another step and I'm inside the shower. A burst of soap. A burst of water. Then shampoo, water, soap, water. In a break from tradition, hot air begins to buffet my body. I stand still for four minutes and fifty-five seconds.

A step forwards into the middle of the room. In a bag is a pile of clothes. I put them on. A loose T-shirt, white. Boxer shorts, white. Baggy trousers, white. This takes exactly one minute and fifty-five seconds.

Turn around and walk back into the middle of the room. A step to the right. Sit down at the table, white of course, upon which a bowl and a glass of milk have been placed. Steam wafts up from the grey goo in the bowl. Filled with enough nutrition and vitamins to keep the body functioning perfectly, without bothering with any details such as taste or texture. I eat and am about to drink the milk when I realise this meal has only taken two minutes and forty-five seconds. I pause, the glass resting on my lip, and count to five. Drink. Get up and walk into the middle of the room. Turn further right and go through the door, which slides open.

My enclosure is huge: you could fit my room into it several times over. It has a tyre swing, a pond, and a small wooden climbing frame. In a corner there is also a bundle of puzzles in case I get bored of physical exercise. The walls are transparent safety glass, apart from a couple of metres of stone wall at the bottom. There is a deep crack in one part but it's never been fixed. Budget cuts. Ten steps take me to my swing. I stand waiting beside it for the remaining four minutes and fifty-five seconds.

Three, two, one... The klaxon squeals again and I get into the swing and begin to drift lazily back and forth. Far off I can hear the crunch of the gates opening and the buzz of voices. As they get closer, I pin a simple smile to my face. I like to hear the sounds of the crowd. When there is no one visiting the zoo, the silence feels oppressive. Compared to that, the hubbub of voices is soothing.

The rest of the morning proceeds as usual. I swing for a bit, occasionally waving at the wide-eyed children who press their faces to the glass. I overhear one, a boy with messy black hair, ask his mother if he can be an exhibit and she snaps 'No!' at him. You can tell it came out harsher than she meant because she immediately repents and tells him he can have a tyre swing at home. After a while I begin to bumble around on the climbing frame, deliberately getting my foot stuck and tumbling off. To my audience of kids, this is the height of comedy and they fall about themselves with laughter. I can't help but smile along with them. It's the only enjoyable part of my life, hearing the children laugh. One little girl, with hair so blonde it is almost white, stands out. Her expression is horrified, a false note amongst the smiles. I leap up and give her a silly bow that puts my nose to the floor, to show her I'm not actually hurt. That works and she giggles. She holds up a metal cube and presses a button on it. A cockerel's crow echoes out. I mimic the sound and she giggles again.

After the morning rush I return to my room for another bowl of goo and a glass of milk. This lasts until 12:05, at which point I once again march out into the enclosure and begin to fiddle with a block puzzle. It isn't the most thrilling viewing but there won't be a lot of people here until late afternoon, so I allow myself some serenity. Then it's after school and a horde of children descend upon the zoo. I feel tired after a little while so I pull my usual trick for these situations. I pretend to get stuck in my tyre swing and wriggle around as though unable to free myself. This keeps the kids entertained and allows me to rest for a little while. The park closes at 18:30. Once the last person leaves, I return to my room. The next couple of hours are spent with one of the keepers, who comes to examine me. I'm poked, prodded, and probed until he is satisfied I'm healthy and then I do my morning routine in reverse. Eat dinner. Undress. Shower. As I step over to my bedding a klaxon goes off and I clamber in. I'm asleep after five minutes.

I wake at 7:44 exactly and go through the usual schedule. I hope to see the blonde girl again but the only group that stares into my enclosure consists of young boys, who chuckle at my antics and play at pushing each other over. After lunch I settle down with my blocks. They have long stopped posing an intellectual challenge, but I find the process of building elaborate structures satisfying.

BANG. I jump, knocking the blocks everywhere, and turn around to find the source of the noise. Three teenagers are slouched on the other side of the glass, dressed in the latest and most expensive fashions. The nearest one, with a blue spiked mohawk and a zippered mackintosh, brings his fist down on the wall. BANG.

'C'mon, do something.' I turn around and start to rebuild my block puzzle. Children are one thing but I don't see any point capering around for some adolescents, especially ones who bang on the wall. BANG. BANG. 'This is so shit. It doesn't do anything.' I take a deep breath and try to carry on with the puzzle but my hands are shaking and none of the pieces seem to fit where I put them.

BANG. BANG. BANG. 'Ha, it's too fucking stupid to fit the blocks together. I heard they were bred dumb but this one is fucking retarded.'

I turn back towards them but I can't quite bring myself to yell back. Don't show aggression to visitors. It's one of the rules. Well, unless that is your act but I'm strictly a docile exhibit. All I do is stare at them through the glass. 'Oh, don't like it?' The one with the blue mohawk turns to his guffawing friends. 'The freak doesn't like it when I bang on the glass.' He gives the wall a kick, causing me to flinch. He turns back, grinning and then begins to speak as though talking to a baby. 'Aw, does the little mutant not like it when I do this?' BANG. He raps his fingers on the glass. My hands begin to clench into fists. 'What are you going to do about it?' He punctuates each word with a bang. 'Nothing. Because. You. Are. Just. A. Caged. Fre–'

I'm across the enclosure in a second, snarling wildly and pounding my fists against the glass. Terror flits across the boy's face for a second and he steps back. I crash against the wall and growl at him. An urge to hurt him, something I've never felt before, fills me. He recovers and begins to grin at me. 'Uh-oh, we upset the monster. Lucky that we're out here.' He throws his arms wide, encompassing the outside world. 'And you're in there.' He taps the glass, the sound lost in my thrashing. He turns around and walks away, slipping a tiny sliver of metal from his pocket. My foot connects with the cracked wall and pain arches up my leg. With it goes all my anger and I slump to the ground. Blue Mohawk holds the device up to his mouth and begins to talk: 'Father, you'll never guess what happened!' The wall I kicked has crumbled slightly, leaving a small hole from my cage into the outside world. I grab a rock and cover it up so that that the keepers won't find it. Then I just curl up on the ground and wait.

The rest of the day flies by in a flurry of suited men and tranquillisers, nervous keepers and yet more tranquillisers. In a brief spurt of consciousness, I hear a snippet of speech: '– have to avoid external influences that might cause a relapse.' Before I can ask what they mean, I'm dragged back into darkness.

I wake at 7:44 exactly. I guess no amount of drugs can overcome a lifetime of routine. Klaxon. Shower. Dress. Eat. I take up my usual position by the tyre swing. The remaining four minutes and fifty-five seconds are tense. After yesterday, I expected to wake chained up or at least suffer a stern reprimand from the head keeper. Surely there must be some consequences for my outburst yesterday. The klaxon sounds again. I mechanically clamber into my swing, trying to detect a change. Frowning, I realise I can't hear the gates opening or the bustle of the crowds. Did they shut down the whole zoo just because of yesterday? If that's the case, I'm in more trouble than I thought. My worries are quickly dispelled when I see a group of children, herded by a frizzy-haired woman, approaching. They point at me but stay silent. I decide to start early and take a backwards roll out of the tyre, complete with over-the-top arm whirling. I hit the floor but still no jot of laughter. I jump up and wave my arms in an attempt to elicit a reaction. That's when I realise. The children are laughing and giggling amongst themselves. They just aren't making a sound. I smack my hand against the tyre and sigh with relief when I hear the muffled thump. They haven't made me deaf. Just turned off the microphones that carry sound into my enclosure. 'External influences', I suppose.

The first day is all right. I do my usual dancing and jumping, and while the lack of reaction is off-putting, I muddle through. The night is when it starts to get to me. I long ago tuned out the hum of traffic and clonk of workmen that filtered in from the outside but now that they are gone, the world feels emptier. I begin to hear the lack of noise. Silence screams. It has a shrill whistle all of its own that you can't avoid by clapping your hands over your ears. There is no escaping it, except with sleep, which comes slowly.

I wake at 7:44 exactly. I wait for the klaxon, for the first time eager to hear it. When it comes, I almost slip off my bedding. The screeching, after so much quiet, feels like a pressure on my head. On the other hand, it also pushes the silence away, a flash of light in the dark. When it stops, I hear the nothing again. I briefly escape it in the shower, again with the rustle of clothes then once more at breakfast, making sure to bring my glass down harder then necessary, revelling in the soft thud. I start to move for the door when I realise that I've been so intent on making noise that I haven't kept to the schedule. I'm not supposed to go outside for another two minutes and forty-three seconds. I fill the time by beating out a rhythm on my glass with my spoon.

I'm swinging listlessly on my tyre when the first group of children arrive. I briefly consider ignoring them but I fear what the keepers will do if I push them further. Plus, the thumps and crashes of me careening around my enclosure are preferable to silence. The blonde girl's group comes again and she seems to enjoy my antics. When I run up and make a scary face at her she jumps and drops her sound cube. She bends to pick it up and my stomach sinks when I realise she has dropped it right by the hole in the wall, unblocked from her side. Her eyes widen when she sees it but she just picks up her toy and then straightens up. Luckily, no one else is paying attention. I give her a grateful look and she just smiles. I don't need any more trouble with the keepers.

Without anything to keep me occupied, the night is bad. It feels as though I'm washing away. I lean my arm down to the floor and tap my knuckles against the floor three times. Tap. Tap. Tap. A brief splash of sound, quickly engulfed.

Tap. Tap. Tap.

Tap. Tap. Tap.

Tap. Tap. Tap.

I wake up at 7:44 exactly. The knuckles on my right hand are torn open, resting in a pool of dried blood. Shower. Dress. Eat. I'm ahead of schedule again, this time by three minutes and seven seconds. I'm about to go back over to the table to tap on my glass again when I stop. Turn back around to the door. A strange impulse grips me. Why keep to the schedule? It might upset the keepers but the long night has quickly worn away my fear of them. I walk over to the door and it slides open as usual. I hesitate on the border and then take a step outside. Then another. I'm in my enclosure two minutes and thirty-three seconds early. I'm not sure whether I'm feeling terrified or elated. I go over to the block puzzles and begin to build a huge tower, as big as I can. The clack of plastic on plastic helps cover up the stillness. I don't realise that I have an audience until I glance around and see a gaggle of children on the other side of the glass. I step away from the blocks and begin to do my usual act. Without sound, the faces of the laughing children stretch and become grotesque, resembling hyenas that have learned to walk on two legs. Anger flares in me and I toss a block at them. It bounces off the wall with a bang. The kids leap back, startled, their mouths miming shock. I turn back around and go back to my tower. I'm left alone for another couple of hours. Twice I knock it down and start again.

I hear boots on grass. It's a small sound but it practically booms. I twist around and see a couple of keepers. One is carrying a medical bag, the other a tranquilliser gun. Before I can move, the gun buzzes and the dart pierces my skin. I fall backwards into my tower and close my eyes amidst the wreckage.

I fade in and out, picking up scattered images and sounds. A man in white leaning over me, shaking his head. The whirring of machinery. The feel of someone pushing open my lips and feeling along my teeth, which brings with it an unpleasant, medicinal taste. A bandage being wrapped around my hand. A small snippet of conversation:

'It's strange, he's been completely fine until a few days ago and I can't find any physical problems, aside from the hand.'

'You know how it is with them, sometimes something inside just unravels.'

'True. If nothing improves soon, we might need to think about termination. It'd be a shame though.'

A part of me tries to focus, aware that the conversation is important but unable to put it together. But my lids are too heavy and I fall back asleep.

The klaxon wakes me. I jerk about, throwing my bedding all over the place in my surprise. That hasn't happened in a long time. I shower, dress, and eat but take my time. I'm only just starting my breakfast when the second klaxon goes off. Eventually I walk out at a leisurely pace and sit down on the climbing frame. The morning crowd of children come by but they wander off quickly when they realise I'm not going to do anything.

One lingers and I realise with a jolt that it's the blonde girl from before. She waves at me and her mouth moves. I try to make out what she is saying but I can't fit words to her lips. I shake my head and point to my ears. She looks confused, silvery eyebrows knitting together, but then beckons me over. I shake my head again. She doesn't understand the problem. She glances back at the rapidly disappearing group of children and beckons again. I don't think she will budge until I go to her. Sighing, I hurry over. She points at the bottom of the wall, where the crack is. I look around quickly but no keepers seem to be watching. She crouches down by it and sticks her hand through the hole. I bend down as well and pull the rock out of the way. Her arm can only just reach through to my side. In her hand is her sound cube. She presses a button and I hear a cow moo. It sounds deafening. I look up at her. She nods and puts the cube down on my side. I reach out and pick it up. It feels used, the surface pitted. She quickly withdraws her hand and stands up. I mouth my thanks at her. She smiles, waves again, and then runs off to rejoin her group.

I retreat back inside my room, despite the fact that I've only been in the enclosure for a couple of hours, and spend the rest of the day playing with the device. It has every animal sound you can think of, barks and roars and growls and whinnies. The menagerie of sound chases the silence away, its tinny whistle drowned out under the sheer variety of noise.

When I hear the whine of the outer doors opening, I panic. The keepers are here to check on me again. If they find the cube, they'll take it away for sure. I look around for somewhere to hide it but my room is spartan, devoid of hidey-holes. The footsteps are coming closer. I pull open my trousers and hold it to my side with the elastic waistband. It's not the best hiding place but under my baggy shirt it's pretty unnoticeable. When the keepers come, I don't try and dodge the tranquilliser dart but stay very still, so that the cube doesn't fall out.

I wake up at... I'm not sure when. My vision is drug smeared. I'm strapped down on a gurney. It takes me a few seconds to realise that I'm being pushed and that the walls aren't just moving of their own accord. Two keepers are talking but I can't make any sense of it.

'A damn shame.'

'Eh, plenty more where that came from.'

A door buzzes. From what I can make out, the room is lined with medical equipment. One of the keepers puts a needle into my arm. Whatever was in it is cold. It feels like my veins are frosting over. Then he mutters something to the other one and they leave the room.

It must be more tranquilliser because I can feel it trying to pull me back into sleep. I try to resist. My arm is strapped down but I can just about stretch my hand out to grasp the sound cube. My fingers close over the cold metal and I sigh with relief. They didn't find it. My sight is getting hazier. I try and press one of the buttons but I can't control my fingers and they slip. My body feels sluggish. My eyes are almost closed now; I can't stay awake much longer. I concentrate as hard as I can and hold my finger over one of the keys. I push down. The sound of an elephant fills the room. I smile, feel the skin across my face ripple. I keep my finger on the button and the sound loops. I can't keep my eyes open.

Everything begins to drift away. First the medical room, then the pressure of my straps, the cool metal of the cube and, finally, the trumpeting of elephants.

Andrew Jury is making his third Fiction Desk appearance with this new story: see also '"Glenda"' in All These Little Worlds, *and 'Exocet' in* The Maginot Line.

Last Night

Andrew Jury

'Are you awake?' Matt asked Laura.

'I'm awake,' Laura told Matt.

'You slept at all?'

'Not a wink.'

Laura looked at the digital clock on her side of the bed. 2:47. When was the last time she had been awake at 2:47? Five years ago? Ten? Most evenings, she was asleep by eleven, midnight at the latest. Even when they had friends round, she was always the first to call it a night. Matt, fuelled by whisky and cigars, could keep going until two or three in the morning, but she never heard him come into the bedroom at the end of the night, only ever felt his mass, his gravitational tug, pulling at her dreams.

Most nights, a nuclear strike wouldn't wake her.

Most nights.

'Do you think we made a mistake?'

'He's not a kid, Laura.'

'He's sixteen years old.'

'Seventeen next month.'

'He's a baby.'

'You should have seen some of the things I got up to when I was his age.'

'Of course, Matt dear.'

'I mean it. There's plenty of stuff I haven't told you about.'

'You've told me everything. And even if you hadn't, I've talked to all the people who knew you before I did. There are no skeletons hiding in your closet.'

'I'm telling you, I was a dark horse. Still am.'

'Really?'

'Who knows? I could've been. Given the chance.'

Matt might always have been the man he was now, but she'd had her moments. When she was a kid, not much older than Josh, the mere sound of her key turning in the lock at two or three in the morning would be enough to spring her parents from their separate bedrooms, like a couple of ageing greyhounds. The two of them would merge together at the top of the stairs, a malign cluster of midlife doubts and anxieties, while Laura, fully charged, the music still banging in her eardrums, the flesh on her perspiring young body glazed by the cool night air, stared up at them, wondering how they had gotten so old, so goddam geriatric.

'Jesus Christ, why do you worry so much? It's not like anything's going to happen to me. I'm just having some fun!'

Yeah... right, she thought now.

'He's a bright kid,' said Matt. 'Got a good head on his shoulders. He won't do anything reckless or stupid.'

'He's sixteen years old. Having a good head on his shoulders doesn't come into it.' *Not when the rest of his body's a festering, hormonal swamp.*

'He's seventeen next month.'

'Say that again, and I'll kill you.'

'All right. He's only sixteen for the next three weeks.'

'Is this supposed to be making me feel better?'

'Would anything I say right now?'

She looked at the clock (2:54) at the same moment Matt laid a hand on her left breast. She let it stay there for a few seconds before gently easing it back across the no-man's-land separating their two sides of the bed.

'Not tonight, Josephine?' he asked, only a little playfully.

When she ignored him, he started to snore. Big comical snores, nothing at all like the high-pitched whistle that actually came shrieking out of his nasal passages when he was asleep. She nudged him in the ribs, told him to cut it out. She wasn't in the mood.

'You can say that again.'

A moment later the lamp on her side of the bed came on.

'What's that supposed to mean?'

He sat up and fumbled around on the bedside table for his spectacles. Swept a lock of greying hair from his forehead. Fifty years old, she thought, and still a handsome man, even at three o'clock in the morning. More importantly, her body continued to crave him, often when she least expected it to; still responded to his touch the way it always had, even after twenty-odd years together. It was a kind of miracle, when you thought about it, and without even quite knowing that she was doing it, her hand reached down for his cock, but he was up and out of the bed a split-second before she could rein him in.

'I need a drink,' he said. 'How about you?'

'Sure,' she said.

He stretched and yawned. He never wore a shirt to bed, and she noticed with pleasure that, aside from some flecks of grey in the hairs on his chest, his hard, tanned torso was that of a man fifteen years younger. Even the sight of those hairs, their contrast to his nut-brown skin, the exceptions to the firm rule of his body, excited her in a way she couldn't fully comprehend.

'Tea? Hot milk?'

'Something stronger,' she said, when really all she wanted was for him to fuck her. To be fucked by her husband.

'How about a brandy? Or whisky?'

'I don't know if we have any.'

'What about that bottle your Uncle Stan gave us for Christmas?'

'Your brother polished it off on New Year's Eve.'

'He did? How did that happen?'

'You were too drunk to stop him.'

'So why didn't you?'

'I tried, and he called me a nine-carat arsehole,' she told him. 'What's more, you agreed with him.'

'He calls everyone that.'

'And do you always agree?'

'Depends how drunk I am,' he said.

'We must have something else.'

'I'll see what I can do.'

The moment he left the bedroom, her libido followed him out of the door... but that was fine, too. Alone, she allowed the sheets to fall from her breasts and looked down at her body. Had it weathered as well as her husband's? She was forty-eight, a couple of years younger than him, an age where her small tits now seemed a blessing rather than a curse. She used to catch Matt occasionally eyeing up the buxom friends she had once envied – used to tease him about it – but now, as their hard racks swelled into matronly middle age, he barely batted an eyelid. More than a handful seems a waste, he used to say to her, back when such things actually mattered, before it turned into just another one of their jokes.

She pulled the covers back up to her chin. Stretched her legs. Curled her toes. Relished the sudden flexing of muscles in her calves. Where was Matt? Had he popped out to the all night offy for an overpriced bottle of Jack D? She told herself not to look at the clock and immediately looked at the clock. 3:03. Three oh three, she thought, and said it out loud. 'Three oh three. Three oh! three. Oh, Three, thou art three past thee...'

She wondered what time it was in New York. In Tokyo. In the Baffin Islands. Josh had recently declared his intention to go backpacking during his 'gap year' in some far-flung, previously war-torn country. They had told him they would discuss it closer to the time, which was their way of saying they hoped the whole idea would go up in smoke long before that discussion ever became a reality. She had never travelled outside the EU. Never been to New York or Tokyo, didn't even know where the Baffin Islands were. Didn't really care. 'Gap year': what did that even mean? What was wrong with taking a year off? Bumming around? Kids today, eh? Everything had to have a meaning. She closed her eyes, waggled her toes, sent her left leg over the invisible border that marked her side of the bed from his side of the bed. Anything to declare, madam? Yeah, I want a full body search... I want you to strip me naked and shove a hand up my... Her passport needed renewing, but she was reluctant to get it done, if only because the photo in the old one was how she imagined she still looked rather than what she actually saw in the mirror each morning. She didn't think the next one would be half as good. In fact, she had it on good authority from her reflection that it would almost certainly be granted an X certificate.

Where the hell was Matt? Suddenly the bed seemed very large. When Josh was small, he would sometimes climb in and insert himself into the precise Josh-sized gap between their two bodies, like the final piece of a perfect jigsaw. Those times, she would always feel sorry for all the future versions of herself, apologise to them in advance, convinced that her life was never going to get any better than this. And she was probably right. Not that her life was so bad now.

Matt appeared in the doorway carrying a tray with two glasses and a bowl of snacks. He was wearing one of Josh's wrinkled T-shirts, which he must have plucked from the clothes horse in the kitchen. This one bore the name of a band their son had liked a couple of years ago, and a list of tour dates on the back. It looked foolish on the body of her fifty-year-old husband, but she supposed that was the point.

'Vodka and orange for the lady,' he said, handing her the glass. 'And a boring old Coke for the gentleman of the house.'

'What took you so long?'

'Took a detour through Flush City.'

He climbed into bed, wedged the snacks between their bodies and took a sip of the coke.

'LCD Soundsystem,' she said, reading his chest.

'You should listen to some of their tracks. They rock.'

'Tracks? You mean songs...'

'My dear, do you have any idea how positively old you sound?'

Matt sometimes liked to play CDs from Josh's collection, usually when their son had his friends round. He said it was because he liked to keep in touch with something he called The Scene, but really her husband was just a wind-up merchant.

'You shouldn't wear his clothes,' she told him.

'You don't think I can pull this off?'

'I wish you would.'

'It doesn't matter. He only ever wears it to bed.'

'Which means you shouldn't.'

She took a sip of the drink.

'Good?' he asked.

'Not bad.'

'Drinking at two in the morning,' he said. 'Some might say you have a problem.'

'It's after three o'clock,' she said, and looked at the clock.

'Stop looking at the clock,' he told her.

'I can't help it,' she said. 'He's my baby boy. And if you say he's nearly seventeen years old, I'll rip that T-shirt off your geriatric body and use it to strangle you with.'

'Quit worrying. He'd have called us if there was a problem.'

'Or he hasn't called us because there *is* a problem.'

'We told him not to call, if you remember. That was the whole point...'

'No, you told him that.'

'And if it was left to you, he'd be wearing a tag until his eighteenth birthday.'

For a moment, the only sound was the crunch of nuts inside Matt's mouth. Then,

'I'm going to call his mobile.'

Matt put a hand on her arm. 'That's precisely what you're not going to do.'

'Are you going to stop me?'

'Yes, I am. With brute physical force, if necessary.'

'I'd like to see you try.'

She took another, longer sip of the vodka as his hand dipped into the bowl of snacks. The sound of nuts and crisps scraping around the porcelain at three in the morning sounded wrong somehow.

He said, 'He mentioned Sierra Leone again.'

'When?'

'A couple of nights ago. As I was driving him to the recital. He seems determined to go through with it.'

'Why didn't you tell me?'

'He asked me not to. He didn't want you to worry.'

She laughed. 'But now it's okay.'

'You're fretting anyway. I thought this particular worry might take your mind off the other one.'

'Or alternatively make me anxious about two things where before I was only anxious about one.'

'Yes, there's that too.' He grabbed a handful of nuts. Flicked them into his mouth one by one. She hated that.

'We could always have sex,' he said. 'Take your mind off Sierra Leone.'

'The moment's gone.'

'It has? When was it ever there?'

'The moment you left the room.'

'That's when I'm at my most irresistible,' he said, and yawned. 'How about a game of chess? We haven't played chess since we were married.'

'We've never played chess. Not once,' she told him. 'We don't even have a board.'

'I still have my old travel set. Magnetic. I used to take it everywhere when I was a kid. The king is about one centimetre high and you use a pair of tweezers to make a move.'

'The sad part is that I actually believe you.'

'In my school, chess club was where all the hot babes used to hang out.'

'Pawn stars,' she said, and took a long swig of the vodka. 'Do you think he's still a virgin?'

'Who?'

'Gary Kasparov,' she said. 'Who do you think? Our son. Josh...'

'I wouldn't have thought so.'

He went to reach for the snacks again, but she pulled his hand out of the bowl. 'Has he said something?'

'To me? No. But if you were to ask me the odds, I'd say it was seventy-thirty in favour of a cherry burst.'

'Is that something you really believe or have you just made it up on the spur of the moment?'

'Call it a gut instinct,' he said. 'Male intuition.'

'Male intuition,' she repeated. 'So when did you lose yours?'

'I've told you all this.'

'Tell me again.'

He cleared his throat, as though he were about to step up to a mike. 'I was twenty-two. Her name was Tracey Bignall. She never knew what hit her.'

She laughed.

'What's so funny?'

'Twenty-two. A postgraduate. How could you go through three years at University without having sex? I mean, what were you doing?'

'What was I doing? Studying.'

'And yet you still didn't get a first.'

'I also masturbated.' He popped another handful of cashews into his mouth. 'Actually, I could have self-loved for England.'

'So who do you think was the lucky girl? Zoe? Or maybe that first one he brought home, the one with the crooked smile...'

'Madeline?'

She nodded.

'It wasn't either of those two.'

'Why not?'

'Because they were more for our benefit than his. A couple of nice girls to put us off the scent.'

'So there's some other girl he doesn't want us to meet... one who isn't Matt and Laura friendly.'

He shrugged.

'Come on, Matt. I know you're holding something back...'

'Well, I've heard him on the phone to someone. A girl – at least, I hope it's a girl.'

'Not that you'd have a problem if it wasn't...'

'Of course not. Not in the sense you mean.' There was a soft pause. 'I've also seen a couple of texts.'

'You've looked at his phone.'

'If he leaves it lying around the way he does, what does he expect? I'm his father. I'll respect his privacy when he's eighteen. Until then, I'm happy for him to labour under the false perception that his personal life is none of our business...'

'For the record, you're a terrible father,' she told him. 'So what do these texts say?'

'Not much. There was some flirting, and a bit of sex talk, playful rather than hardcore; stuff he probably picked up from the TV or off the internet.'

'You've seen this girl?'

'In the flesh? Only from a distance, when I dropped him off at school one morning and hung around for a couple of minutes. You know, the way you do when you're checking up on your kids. And there were some pictures on his phone.' She must have pulled a face without knowing it, because he quickly added, 'Not those kind. Just head and shoulders. *Tres* tasteful'

'So what does she look like?' she asked him. 'Elvira, Mistress of the Dark?'

'She's dark all right, but dusky. Possibly some Mediterranean blood in her past. Actually, she's a bit of a stunner...'

'But?'

'But you only have to look at her face to know that there's an edge to her.'

She didn't like the sound of that. An edge. No, she didn't like that at all. 'Do you think she'll be at this party?'

'She probably is the party.'

'Matt!'

'How should I know? She probably is. So what? We can't wrap the kid up in cotton wool. He's almost sev– he's sixteen years old,' he corrected himself. 'A sixteen-year-old today is equivalent to a twenty-year-old in old money.'

'Your money maybe.'

She snatched a handful of peanuts out of the bowl. She had known all along that these would be the worst years, when he was neither man nor boy, but some hybrid of the two, as if the young Josh was being slowly absorbed by a phlegmatic, sharp-eyed stranger who bore only a passing resemblance to the child she'd cherished for the first fifteen years of his life. She could almost hear the laughter of her younger self, the one who had snuggled up to her baby boy in this very bed – what? – ten minutes ago. *See, the only thing I have to worry about is croup and colic. No textual flirting, no dusky Mediterranean babes with an edge to contend with here.*

But Josh was essentially a good kid. Like any teenager, he had his tantrums and his strops, his bubonic mood swings, his bouts of patricidal anguish (though not so many as she might have anticipated all those years ago). But unlike Laura, whose rebellion against her own parents was a savage, daily re-enactment of every grievance she'd ever harboured against them (and didn't they like to remind her of it during every telephone conversation and on every visit home?), Josh's outbursts always concluded in a spirit of conciliation rather than confrontation. He was, according to her husband, a born mediator; a kid planning to major in psychology, assuming he made it through his gap year in one piece.

Gap year. Sierra Leone. Jesus.

She looked at the clock.

3:14.

'Stop looking at the clock,' Matt told her.

'Her name,' she said to him. 'The Girl with the Edge. What's her name?'

'I don't know.'

'I can't believe you didn't tell me about her.'

'It's because I knew you'd react like this if I did.'

'Like what? Like some hysterical, mollycoddling control freak.'

'Don't put words in my mouth, Laura.'

She snorted. 'I'm surprised you've got room for any in there.'

'What's that supposed to mean?'

She grabbed a handful of nuts from the bowl and jammed them into her mouth. Made a sound like a pig achieving orgasm, or what she imagined that sounded like. Matt stared at her for a moment, and then, without speaking a word, climbed out of bed and strode out of the bedroom. She heard his footsteps going down the stairs and a few moments later imagined him in the front room playing solitaire on his laptop in the dark, his unshaved, fifty-year-old face transformed into a grainy death-mask by the glow of the monitor.

'Fuck off then,' she said, both meaning it and not meaning it, and closed her eyes. Stars sparkled beneath her lids, galaxies and constellations created and destroyed in the blink of an eye. That meant a migraine was coming on; the kind that originated as a dull throb in the middle of her forehead, and would eventually lead to her skull feeling as if it had been hollowed out with a rusty teaspoon. She tried to picture herself falling asleep, to imagine it in the way those 'soothing voices' on the self-help CDs Matt had once bought her encouraged you to. *Guided Meditation. Deep Relaxation.*

Snoozing for Dummies. The same fuzzy language, delivered in the same slushy tones. New Age saccharine for the soul. Still, it was worth a try.

S-l-e-e-p, she said the word in her mind, dreamily, distantly. Sleep... perchance to dream. Anxious dreams...

Bollocks!

(Put on the light. Turn it back off again. Look at the clock. 3:21.)

She went over to the window and opened the curtains. An ordinary street, she thought, in an ordinary suburban town, as the words of some old song from the eighties began swimming around in her head. She saw a blue light flickering off the walls of the darkened houses opposite, thought for a moment that it was the pulse of a house alarm, before the sight of a police car coming down the street, its lights flashing but its siren turned off, caused her heart to skip a beat. A flashing light signified official police business, but the absence of a siren suggested that the incident was already over; that they were in the aftermath of some terrible event, a tragedy. She closed her eyes and saw two officers coming to her door: an old 'un and a young 'un. The older one takes a step towards her. He has a kind, sad face and a moustache like her father's. Maybe he *is* her father. Are you Laura King, mother of Josh King? She's standing there in her favourite bathrobe and a pair of fluffy slippers she doesn't even own, clutching the alarm clock in her hands. 'Officer, don't you know it's 3:21 in the morning?' she says, and points to the digital readout on the clock. The young PC peers over his older colleague's shoulder. He's talking into the radio on his shoulder, the way they do in Police dramas on the TV. She expects him to remind her of Josh, but he looks more like Matt when she first met him; Matt who is nowhere to be seen, who's still trying to beat his own high score on

Solitaire. 'You worry too much. He's almost seventeen,' he will later tell her through a mouthful of nuts.

She opened her eyes. The patrol car slowed down as it approached their house – at least, it slowed down in her imagination – before continuing to the end of the street and disappearing from her line of vision. She let out her breath again. Felt something akin to relief. But it didn't last long. Somewhere out there, her boy was in some other house, maybe sitting on the stairs and talking to a girl with an edge to her as she goads Josh into drinking shots and taking a few tokes of some substance that is still vaguely illegal. Maybe the patrol car was on its way to that very house. And into her mind flashed another scenario: Josh not dead, but arrested. Her and Matt at the police station, talking to the same PC with the same lugubrious face and the moustache like her father's, but now his tone is less compassionate as he says, 'Let this be a warning to your son.' Or worse: 'We've decided to make an example of this young man, Mrs King. He can forget about university. His future. Sierra Leone. Master Joshua is going down for a very long time.'

Oh my God. That's terrible. But...

Sierra Leone.

Every cloud has a silver lining, she thought.

She returned to the bed and sat cross-legged on top of the sheets, the way she had as a student. No chance of sleep now. *I'll go to sleep, if I can,* she thought. *If I cannot, I'll rail against all the first-born of Egypt.* What was that? Shakespeare? The Bible? Her mind was like the top drawer of her grandmother's sideboard: full of junk that no one had thought about in years or could have any possible use for. If only you could detach her head from her shoulders, tip it upside down and give it a shake, the way she and her mother had tipped out that drawer a few days after her grandmother's death, what kind of crap would spill out onto the floor? Snippets from plays, poems and films, most of them decades old; lyrics of old pop songs, wrongly remembered; random scenes from a life in no particular order: A stranger's tanned and hirsute hand on her pre-pubescent shoulder. A dead crab on a beach. Five-year-old Josh lying on his stomach with his hands behind his back, pretending to swim like an eel. The landmark stuff, the things that were supposed to matter: graduation, her first job, their wedding, Josh's birth, his first day at school, her and Matt's thirtieth, fortieth, fiftieth birthdays. All of it was so well documented, so endlessly recycled, that the real feelings she had experienced at the time were no longer detachable from her various states of mind on each occasion she had replayed them. It was as if some pure, authentic truth lay buried beneath a stratum of false emotions. And not for the first time, she thought how delving into a middle-aged mind is like working on an archaeological dig; how the stuff you find first, the rusty coins and shards of broken ceramic sticking out the ground, are always the least interesting. But more often than not, that's all that there is left... unless you have the patience to dig elsewhere.

Downstairs, she heard the toilet flush again, followed by the sound of Matt noisily clearing his throat. For the past couple of years, he had started getting up for a piss two or three times a night, scrambling out of the bed at three and six o'clock in the morning, his fingertips brushing one of her exposed breasts as he set off on another journey to Flush City. A few minutes later, she would feel his cold hand, unwashed, snaking across her back; his piss-stained fingertips inventorying the knobs of her spine. Sorry to disturb you, he would whisper into her ear, even though she was not really awake, simply drifting in the tide of her own inner Styx. Those were the times when he could have confessed anything to her – 'I'm having an affair', 'I'm into women's fashion', 'I flash ageing housewives in the park' – and she would have only thought without ever remembering, *Who cares? It's three past three in the morning. Three Oh! Three. Go back to sleep.*

She closed her eyes and tried, in vain, to recall one single item that had fallen out of her grandmother's drawer that day. Nothing came to mind, not a single thimble or hand-embroidered doily. All she could remember was wanting to cry, to feel about her grandmother the same way children felt about their grandparents in so many of the books she had read in her youth, and how this desire had expressed itself as a dull ache in the centre of her chest, like a migraine of the soul. Her Gran was a good person, kind and attentive, a woman who always wore a pinafore in every room of the house (even the bedroom?) and baked cakes that tasted like no subsequent cake she had ever tasted, but she inspired no great emotions in the young Laura, and her drawer was so full of old lady crap that even her mother wouldn't remember any of it.

Her mobile phone emitted a couple of sad little beeps, hauling her back to the present ('Mobile phones!' her grandmother had exclaimed shortly before she died as Laura jabbed away at the rubber keys on her brick-like Motorola. 'Whatever will they think of next?'). For a moment, she thought it was a text from Josh – *pissed, stoned, about to get laid. how r u?* – but it was just a low battery warning. She plugged the phone into the charger in the wall socket, and it made a jaunty little sound, a kind of digital hip-hip-hooray!, as a picture of Josh, impossibly young, appeared briefly on the screen. She thought about how the screensaver on her laptop rotated pictures from their family album every thirty minutes, but the one on her phone had always been of Josh aged seven, his young face smiling up at her every time she made or received a call, gone in the blink of an eye, like a subliminal blast from the past. Remember me?

She moved over to the dressing table and stared at herself in the mirror, something she never did after ten at night unless, like now, her contact lenses were out. Squinting back at her was a blurry forty-eight-year-old HR manager who couldn't get to sleep because they (Matt) had let their (his) son stay out at an all-night party. She wondered what had happened to that girl who had driven everyone she knew to distraction. Where had she gone, that other girl with an edge to her? What would she say to her if she was sitting here right now? Would she say anything? Or would the two of them just stare at each other, at a loss for words, one refusing to acknowledge what she had become, the other only too aware of everything she'd never be again.

The only thing she would tell her younger self was this: leave my son alone.

Hard to believe that she had once been a girl of sixteen, a young student of twenty-two, an ambitious woman of thirty; that she had once written poems using a fountain pen, carried out charitable acts she couldn't really afford to, slept with men whose names and faces she couldn't remember. Hard to believe she had ever been childless and fearless, Matt- and Josh-less; even harder to believe that if this was the midpoint of her life, she would have to remain on this mortal coil a couple of decades longer than her Gran.

The truth was that she was a forty-eight-year-old HR manager who could still write poetry on her iPad, if she wanted to, still carry out charitable acts, all of which she could afford to, and still sleep with men, even those whose names and faces she would sadly remember. It wasn't beyond the realms of possibility… even that last part. There were still credible suitors, if 'suitor' was still a word. There was the company's new head of finance, Tony, fifty-something, freshly divorced, and constantly on the prowl. Tony, who was always popping into her office for something that could wait, some matter of only the slightest importance: a laugh, a word, a hole punch. Vain Tony, some of the older women, the ones for whom his patois was merely playful, called him behind his back, because he wore snappy suits and scheduled one-to-one meetings with his own reflection (so they said) and had been voted the Sexiest Man Over Forty in a poll by all the company's female employees (and two gay males) under thirty. She could sleep with him tomorrow, if she wanted to. Go to his apartment (not flat) in a newly fashionable area of town and be with Tony while he watched himself having sex with her.

Yes, she could do that, if she wanted to, even if there was more chance of her writing a good poem or performing an act of sheer altruism before such a thing actually happened.

So she went downstairs and found Matt sitting in front of the computer playing Spider Solitaire in his boxer shorts, exactly as she knew she would. She came up behind him and put her hands on his shoulders, counting the seconds until he forgave her for comparing the sound of his eating peanuts to that of a pig achieving orgasm. One... two... three... and then the muscles in his shoulders relaxed, the back of his head was resting against her breasts, and the half-finished game of Solitaire was a distant memory, though she noticed he had surreptitiously clicked 'Save Game' first. Not that it mattered. Not when they had both recently passed the mark where they had been married to each other for more than half their lives. ('It's my fifty per cent day,' Matt had said to her upon reaching that particular landmark, before handing her a gold locket containing within it two tiny portraits of their younger selves.) Someday, years from now, the percentage of time spent apart from each other would be so infinitesimal that it would appear to be little more than the remainder to some grand equation of their lives together.

Express Matt not married to Laura as a fraction of their lives spent untogether. So if he wanted to 'Save Game' prior to her screwing his brains out, that was fine... just as she knew he would be fine about her only reason wanting to screw his brains out was because it was the best way she could forget that it was 3:37 in the morning, and that her son was out for the night, in a house she had never visited, in the arms of a strange girl with an edge to her.

Not that she would tell him that, of course.

It's rare to find a good short story written entirely through dialogue: finding a pace that works both for the rhythm of the narrative and as convincing dialogue is tricky. In 'Love Stops at Ten Metres', Ian Shine shows us how it's done.

Love Stops at Ten Metres

Ian Shine

'And what if he asked you to jump off a cliff, Sarah? Would you do that too?'

'I might.'

'What?'

'I might jump off a cliff if he asked me too.'

'What do you mean, you *might*?'

'Well, it would depend on the cliff: on the size, on the location, on what lay the bottom. And on what he'd do if I did it.'

'Stop being stupid.'

'I'm not being stupid.'

'Yes you are.'

'No I'm not. Wouldn't you jump off a cliff for Dad, if he really wanted you to?'

'If your dad wanted me to jump off a cliff, he wouldn't be much of a husband, would he? Or a father.'

'What if he said, "Jump off this cliff or I'll divorce you"?'

'Sarah!'

'What if the cliff was only one metre high? Would you do it?'

'If it was only one metre high, it wouldn't be much of a cliff, would it?'

'Just imagine. For me.'

'What's the point of saying I'd jump off a cliff if it's only one metre high?'

'Mum!'

'Okay, okay. I'd do it. Happy now?'

'Two metres?'

'Oh, for Pete's sake.'

'Is that a yes?'

'Yes, okay. I don't see why not.'

'Three?'

'Erm, yes, I suppose.'

'Ten metres?'

'Sarah!

'Come on, Mum.'

'Ten metres... how high is that?'

'Dunno. Off the roof of the house maybe.'

'I'd break my legs.'

'They'd heal.'

'Not when you're as old as me, they wouldn't. Things take longer to heal when you get older.'

'In that case, would you be prepared to have a permanent disability for Dad?'

'Sarah! What's the matter with you?'

'You jump ten metres, you have crutches for the rest of your life, but you've also got Dad.'

'Oh come on. This is completely unrealistic. I would never be faced with that choice.'

'Crutches or no Dad?'

'Okay, okay. I suppose if I had to, I'd do it.'

'Okay. Now twenty metres?'

'Oh stop it.'

'No, come on. Twenty metres. Two broken legs and a broken neck. Three months in hospital, probably a wheelchair.'

'No no no. I wouldn't do it.'

'So that's it? Ten metres? Love stops at ten metres? Couldn't you stretch to eleven or twelve?'

'Oh God, this is ridiculous. Look, I'd maybe do twelve, okay? Happy? Now, let's stop this stupid talk. I'm not at all impressed by what's happened, and I don't think your father will be either. Do you know...'

'Do you think Dad would be happy that you'd only jump ten metres for him, or *maybe* twelve?'

'What?'

'If I told him, what do you think he'd think?'

'We're not talking about...'

'Do you think he'd jump more? Thirteen metres? Fourteen metres? Twenty metres?'

'Sarah!'

'I think he might.'

'Look, just listen to...'

'I think he'd be very disappointed to find out he's not worth a broken neck to you; that you wouldn't be prepared to spend a few months in hospital and be confined to a wheelchair just so you could spend the rest of your life with him.'

'We're not...'

'I'm going to tell him.'

'Don't you dare!'

'I'm going to.'

'No!'

'I am!'
'Don't, Sarah. Please.'
'Why not?'
'I'm begging you, Sarah. Don't tell him.'
'Well, I might have to tell him.'
'What do you mean, you might have to tell him?'
'Well.'
'Oh God, Sarah, look. Please don't tell him. I'll do anything.'

There are people who say that 'section spinning' in roulette is genuinely possible, and there are people who say that it isn't. You can decide for yourself whether Warwick Sprawson's story resolves this controversy or not...

The System

Warwick Sprawson

I try not to think about it. It's like walking down stairs or riding a bike: if you think too much you'll fuck it up.

I take the ball, push the roulette wheel and flick the ball around the track in the opposite direction. The red and black numbers blur and the casino's bright lights gleam off the wheel's chrome spokes. I roll my shoulders, trying to dispel the tension that's built waiting for Lee.

'Last bets,' I call.

The only customer at my table is a pale, blinkless man slouched on his stool like a melted candle. He peers furtively into a dog-eared notebook then dolefully plops a few more chips onto the green baize. I look around for Lee. He should be here by now.

Like Lee, Blinkless is a regular in the casino's Las Vegas room, though, as far as I can recall, I've never dealt to him before.

'No more bets.' I sweep my arms over the table as the ball slows and pings musically across the wheel's spokes before coming to rest.

Zero. Bang on target. I place the dolly on the winning number with a surge of triumph.

Dealing roulette is the one thing I've ever been good at. I don't have a girlfriend, I'm not witty, I have few friends, I hate sport and I'm not artistic... but damn, I run a good game of roulette. Not only do you need to be an enforcer, keeping control of big games where arms seethe across the table like tentacles, but you also need the brains to calculate complex payouts.

What's thirty-five times four, plus seventeen times six, plus eight times seven, plus two times eleven?

Too slow. Three hundred and twenty.

Lots of dealers have the basic skills, but few turn dealing into an art. I'm not normally a graceful person, but years of spinning, clearing chips and delivering payouts has allowed me to refine my motions until they are as smooth and precise as tai chi in a park.

I sweep Blinkless's losing bets towards me using a gentle breaststroke motion, then use the back of my hand to brush the chips into the maw of the chipping machine.

Blinkless has lost five hundred dollars in twenty minutes. He seems to bet with a system; most regulars do. He chews his pencil and jots in his notebook. The book's rumpled pages are full of scrawled calculations, sketches of wheels and columns of numbers.

'Place your bets.'

Lee hooks his leg over a stool and throws a wad of notes on the table. He rolls up the sleeves of his blue shirt to reveal his colourful tattoos and turns a smile on Blinkless. 'Any luck tonight, Chief?'

Blinkless shies away, hiding his notebook from view.

I count the notes onto the table. It's all there. Ten thousand dollars, half of it mine.

'One hundred dollar chips,' Lee says. 'I'm feeing lucky.'

How can he sound so confident when I can hardly keep my hands from shaking? It's just one of the reasons I admire him so much.

I take five stacks of black hundred dollar chips and slide them across the table.

I got to know Lee at the two-dollar tables. At least twice a week he'd wander in and lay down a few hundred dollars saying something like, 'Plumbing, the last frontier of cash-in-hand.' Unlike most regulars he was sociable, always up for a chat; a welcome distraction on long, quiet nights. It didn't matter whether he won or lost, he was always in a good mood, joking with the waitresses, speculating on the backgrounds of other punters, taking the piss out the casino's kitsch décor and cheesy background music. He said he liked the way I dealt.

Blinkless sneaks a peek in his notebook and doles out chips. Lee confidently puts a chip straight up on zero and further chips on thirty-two, fifteen, nineteen, four, and twenty-one: the numbers to the right of zero on the wheel. He places further bets on twenty-six, three, thirty-five, twelve, and twenty-eight: the numbers to the left of zero on the wheel. This is called a neighbour bet. It's a simple, undetectable plan, but my heart still kicks hard in my chest.

I dry my fingertips on the leg of my trousers and send the ball zinging around the wheel. 'Last bets.'

Blinkless plonks down a few more chips. Lee leans back on his stool and orders a bourbon and coke from a passing waitress.

The ball orbits smoothly around the wheel with a gentle scouring sound.

'No more bets.' I wave my hands across the table as the ball plinks and plunks across the frets.

I swallow and glance at the wheel. 'Twenty-eight, black.'

I place the dolly on Lee's black chip and sweep away the losing bets. Blinkless has lost as usual. I slide Lee over his winnings: thirty-five black chips. Revenge really is sweet.

Blinkless looks dolefully at his few remaining chips. This is one of the reasons I hate the casino. It presents itself as a glamorous destination for sophisticated people, yet it gets the bulk of its money from people like Blinkless: addicts in tracky-dacks. The casino thinks its moral responsibility ends with a gambling helpline poster in the toilets.

Lee takes five chips and uses his thumb to roll one chip off the front of the stack and flip it to the rear. It's a deft trick, made even more difficult by all the rings he wears on his fingers. When we meet later, I'll have to ask him how it's done.

'Place your bets.'

When I was training to be a dealer, back when I was bright eyed and had a full head of hair, they showed us surveillance footage of people trying to swindle the casino. The footage mostly showed hapless punters trying to slip a chip onto the table after the fall of the ball, but there were also clips of dealers trying to steal as well. The dealers' ruses were slightly more sophisticated, such as passing a stack of two-dollar chips with a hundred-dollar chip hidden among them to an accomplice, or else slipping a palmed chip into a sleeve or pocket. It didn't matter how sophisticated the scam, each clip ended with a visit from a black-suited security guard. The message was clear: we have twenty cameras focused on each table; you shifty bastards better not even think about shafting us.

The casino doesn't realise a lack of trust provokes a lack of loyalty.

Lee places the neighbour bet centred on twenty-eight. His drink comes and he chats easily with the waitress. He is often at the casino with a beautiful girl, a different one each time. Blinkless makes a calculation in his notebook and lays down his chips until he only has three left.

The other reason I hate the casino is more personal. Hundreds of dealers work here, but I'm one of the best. So why am I still dealing shitty tables in the Las Vegas room after ten years? Lesser dealers, with lesser experience, are earning twice as much working in the VIP rooms. I should be up there too.

Once a year it gets explained to me at my performance review. As well as cameras on every table, they also monitor the number of spins, and my spin rate isn't high enough. As one pit boss explained, 'You average twenty spins an hour. That's thirty-three percent below your performance target. Don't worry about making it look beautiful, just start spinning faster.'

I'm a professional. I'm not going to spin up every two minutes like a robot. I'm proud of my work, even if they aren't.

I take the ball and spin up again. I love the sound of the ball whizzing around the wheel, the way it changes pitch as it slows and the satisfying clunks as it tumbles across the wheel.

'Twenty-six, black.'

Blinkless loses. We win.

And it's undetectable. There is no fast fingerwork to be caught on camera. No hushed conversation between conspirators. It just looks like luck.

Back when I was training, the instructor mentioned some veteran dealers were able to hit the same section of wheel each spin. I pictured the ball rotating forty or fifty times one way, and the wheel rotating a similar number of times in the opposite direction. He had to be joking. It would be impossible to spin the ball and the wheel with the exact force required to land the ball on the same section of wheel each spin. I smiled quizzically at the instructor, not sure if this was some kind of roulette initiation, like an apprentice being sent for a left-handed hammer.

Lee incorporates our winnings into the rampart of chips building before him.

'Place your bets.' I unload some chips from the chip-stacker and arrange them neatly in the bank while Lee places the neighbour bet around twenty-six.

Blinkless plonks down his three remaining chips. I'm reaching for the ball when he speaks. 'This game's rigged.'

His voice is clear and sharp. It's a shock to hear him speak, wrong somehow, like one of those mute TV puppets piping up after a lifetime of silence.

I recover enough to give my standard reply. 'The game's not rigged because it doesn't need to be rigged. The odds just aren't in your favour.'

Blinkless stands up and shakes his notebook at me. 'It's rigged, I know it's rigged. I just can't quite prove it.'

Lee turns on his stool and looks at Blinkless steadily. 'Shut the fuck up,' he says. 'You're speaking shit.'

Blinkless hunches into his shirt as if trying to disappear. Lee gives him a final glare then turns back to the table and takes a sip of his drink.

I take a deep breath and spin the wheel, but immediately know I've pushed harder than normal. I try to compensate by spinning the ball slightly harder, but know this spin is purely chance.

'Five, red.' Almost directly opposite twenty-six on the wheel. Lee gives a sound between a groan and a growl, and makes the sound a second time when he sees Blinkless has landed a split.

Blinkless drags his stool further away from Lee and sits down. He accepts his seventeen chips thoughtfully and studies the cover of his notebook for a long moment before shoving it deep into the pocket of his tracksuit pants.

I remove the dolly from the winning number. 'Place your bets.' I glance at Lee. He seems unperturbed by the loss. We had spoken about this. The occasional loss was to be expected; sometimes the ball can hit the right section of the wheel but bounce along the frets for longer than usual. As long as we stay ahead in the long run.

'I still think the game is rigged.' Blinkless watches Lee lay his bets. 'They have magnets beneath the wheel.' When Lee finishes laying his bets, Blinkless places his own.

I suddenly get the shakes. They start at my knees and run up my legs to jangle my spine. Until now I had just gone along with everything, but now I realise this isn't just a dealing exercise, it's stealing; and more than that, I can't afford to lose. My share of the kitty was cash-advanced on my credit card. What the hell am I doing?

I take a couple of deep breaths, stretch my fingers and spin, hardly even looking at the wheel. The spin feels natural, the ball seeming to roll for the perfect length of time, but it lands on eighteen: outside the neighbour bet.

'Yes!' Blinkless pumps his arm. He has another split.

I sweep away the losing bets, the black chips seeming heavy in my hands, and pay Blinkless.

Lee's rampart is reduced, though overall we are still up. I try to give him a look, or as much of a look as I can with so many cameras covering the table. I catch his eye and twitch my head from side to side.

Lee cuts down a pile of chips then stacks them back up. He spots a waitress and orders another drink. His smile is as easy as ever. He lays bets around the eighteen.

'Aren't you going to say "Place your bets"?' asks Blinkless.

'Place you bets,' I repeat mechanically.

Trying to spin a section of the wheel started as just another challenge. I wanted to test the rumour. At first I concentrated on regulating my spin: the same push of the wheel and flick of the ball every time. After a month I was ready to give up. While my spins felt uniform, the winning numbers remained stubbornly random. But I didn't become a good dealer by not persisting, so I experimented with different spins, a little harder and a little softer than normal, still seeking consistency from spin to spin. After three months I found a spin that sometimes hit the same section of wheel. Initially the ball often skittered to another section before coming to rest, but, buoyed by my progress, I redoubled my efforts. Little by little my accuracy improved, until after about five months of effort I finally mastered it, culminating in spinning the number three fives times in a row.

That was the night I ran into Lee in the Rage Bar. I sometimes dropped into the bar for a couple of beers after work, especially if I had been dealing a big game. It was the first time I had seen Lee outside of the casino and it was strange not to be separated by the width of a roulette table. He was just as friendly as usual, insisting on buying me a beer and laughing at my casual clothes. Perhaps I had a few more beers than normal: as well as perfecting my spin I had had my performance review.

At work I had to be circumspect when chatting to Lee, but at the bar I could tell him what I really thought about the casino. I wasn't surprised to learn he shared my feelings about the casino's greed. 'They're leeches,' he said, 'Leeches. Someone should take them down.' Then he put a hand on my shoulder and said seeing me spin the five threes had given him an idea.

'You going to spin or what?' It's Blinkless again, twitching with excitement.

The next spin feels good, though maybe I'm a touch heavy on the wheel. Still, as the ball circuits I feel hopeful. 'Last bets.'

The ball rattles and I glance at the wheel. 'Nineteen, red.'

We lose again, but Blinkless's luck has definitely changed. He is straight up on nineteen and receives his thirty-five chip payout with the makings of a smile.

Lee fiddles with his chips, continuing his nifty thumb roll trick. Why would a plumber wear so many rings? Wouldn't they catch on things?

'Place your bets,' says Blinkless and leans over the table with a handful of chips. Lee places the neighbour bet once more.

I can still do this. I close my eyes and imagine a graceful flick and a smooth spin. Just like I've done a million times before.

But the spin feels wrong. I'm too keyed up; I've flicked the ball too hard. It runs for longer than usual and drops on twenty-two, black.

We lose, Blinkless wins again: two chips straight up on twenty-two for a seventy chip payout. Even with five-dollar chips it's still a three-hundred-and-fifty-dollar win.

I pray for Lee to take the remaining chips and cash out, but he finishes his drink and leans forward to bet again. He looks grim, scolding, as if teaching me a lesson. But it's his money too. Why would he stay?

I try and regain my groove, but the pattern continues. Lee loses while Blinkless maintains his freakish run of good luck. Their piles of chips reverse, Blinkless gaining while Lee's pile erodes, eleven chips per spin, first down to three stacks, then two, then one. After each spin I pray for Lee to leave, to take our remaining chips and cash out. But he stays, obstinately losing more than a thousand dollars a spin, like he doesn't even care about the money.

Lee places his last eleven chips on the table, doggedly maintaining the neighbour bet around the previous winning number.

'Last bets,' I croak.

Blinkless is energised. He places handfuls of bets, always avoiding the numbers Lee selects. Lee places his final chip and pushes up from the table to stand. He looks severe. I realise it's a look that seems natural for him, more natural than all his jokes and smiles.

The ball races around the track. The wheel glitters beneath the lights.

'Seventeen, black.' I place the dolly on Blinkless's pile of chips.

Lee looks at me. His eyes have volume and weight.

'Sorry,' I murmur.

I begin sweeping away the losing bets. I try to calculate Blinkless's payout, but the number won't come.

Tania Hershman has published two volumes of short stories: My Mother Was An Upright Piano: Fictions *and* The White Road and Other Stories. *The following story is the winner of the 2013 Fiction Desk flash fiction competition.*

A Call to Arms

Tania Hershman

'Fifteen-love,' the carer said, and served again. The old man stared hard at the TV screen. The ball came towards him and he willed his arm to move.

'Thirty-love,' the carer said.

'Oh dear,' said the old man.

'Never mind,' she said, and served again.

This time the old man's arm did twitch and wobble, but the ball just sank sadly onto bright green grass.

'Forty-love,' the carer said.

In the third game, the old man finally made contact: satisfying twang of ball on racket. Went into the net.

'Well done!' the cheerful carer said.

'Gosh,' the old man said, and brought a hand up to his forehead, wiped it down.

They played till teatime. The carer switched it off and when the giant screen went dark the old man's world turned back to grey and yellow.

'Tennis!' he said. 'Well.'

'Wonderful!' the cheerful carer said, and wheeled him to the living room.

The old man held his tea cup, looked around for someone near. On his left, but that one wasn't much for conversation, she was gone already.

He took a sip and then said loudly:

'Tennis. Just played a game. Still doing it, you know. You can.'

No one spoke. A cough from somewhere, shouting in the corner where some poor soul was being made to eat.

'I did it in my chair,' he told the room, which wasn't listening. 'Didn't need much else, it's all on telly now. You move your arm and somehow it just knows you've done it.'

He stopped for breath, took another sip of tea and reached out for a biscuit.

'Imagine what could be,' he said. 'I don't mean golf or football. My grandkids, they point their arms and shoot at dragons, rescuing princesses. All that bang-bang.'

Bang-bang, and on that screen inside his head it all went muddy red and brown and he was there again.

'Imagine,' he said softly, 'if they did war that way too. No guns or things like that. Just wave your arms about a bit, sign a treaty, off you go.'

That night the old man had his dream, bombs exploding, mud and blood and thunder all around. He was calling to his mates: 'It's not real! Don't worry!' Waved his arms, but no one heard him. 'It's just make-believe!' he shouted till his voice was gone. But it ended just the same. It always ended just the same.

A very short story from Fiction Desk newcomer Gavin Cameron...

A Big Leap

Gavin Cameron

I don't know exactly how small you are, I think I might be about three thousand times bigger than you. It must be really horrible being your size. When you jump through the grass it must be like going through a forest, and the nettles must sting you if you're not careful. The sky probably looks even further away to you. Do you have a bedroom? You could have a glass of milk and an afternoon nap when you get tired.

You'd probably like to be a bit bigger. If you were the same size as me, you'd be able to run over the grass and go a lot further. You could play football, or ride a bike, or we could even get you some clothes, maybe a T-shirt and some jeans and a pair of new trainers and a hat if you wanted one. Can you swim? A puddle must seem like a swimming pool to you, but the leisure centre probably wouldn't let you in, even if you were my size. And I know Mum wouldn't let you sit at the table because she hates creepy-crawly things so you might have to get your own dinner.

I don't know what I'd call you if you were a girl. I'd call you Graham if you were a boy, so you'd be Graham the grasshopper. I'd get a collar with your name on it like a dog and tell everyone you were mine.

If you were the size of an elephant, I could ride you. We'd go down to the shops for sweets and we could patrol the library and tell noisy people they had to be quiet or we would throw them out. On a Saturday, we'd go out for the whole day and go over the hills and see people in other countries and they would give us little wooden things to take home with us, but we'd still stop for sweets on the way back. Maybe you'd even be able to fly and when it got dark, you could take us all the way up to the moon, and we could play there for a bit, then land back in our back garden, but you'd have to be really quiet because Mr Parker next door doesn't like noise.

I think you'd like to be me but I don't think I'd like to be you. You're just an ornament so you can't move unless we move you but I can move anywhere I like. Oh well, at least you'll be here later. I'll come and talk to you again after dinner.

With this story, and 'Faith' in our anthology The Maginot Line *Ian Sales appears to be becoming our resident sf author. Apparently one journal rejected the following story because 'everybody knows that Neil Armstrong and Buzz Aldrin didn't die on the moon'.*

The Last Men in the Moon

Ian Sales

1969

They look like ghosts, blurred and oddly proportioned figures in white, moving in and out of shadow. One of them waves and bounces in slow motion, rising up into the air as if filled with gas, then gently falling to settle on the grey sand. Jimmy hugs his knees and shivers: only eight years old, but he can feel history thick in the air.

It's four o'clock in the morning and only the flickering of the television screen lights the living room. His parents woke him fifteen minutes earlier, and all three in their dressing gowns trooped downstairs and settled before the twenty-four-inch black-and-white Rediffusion. Mother and Father are behind him now, sitting on the edge of the settee, as intent as he on the fuzzy picture on the screen.

The view pans away, revealing a colourless land of sharp rocks and smoothly undulating folds. Jimmy has lived this moment in the months leading up to the launch, the days leading up to the landing; the poor picture cannot spoil his excitement. The men on the screen are on another world, and he wants to be with them so badly his surroundings are forgotten. The cone of black and white, of light and darkness, in which he sits cross legged is all the world he will acknowledge.

Rendered monochrome by the television's light, the living room of this A-frame house, its G-Plan furniture, is forgotten. The settee with its spindly legs of polished beech, its upholstery of orange wool; and the circular rug beneath him, a roundel of umbers and browns. Outside, a lawn slopes down to a meandering tarmacadam road, where a line of silver birches marks the end of the drive. It might as well be an alien planet, because:

Jimmy is on the Moon.

He is watching Neil Armstrong and Edwin 'Buzz' Aldrin as they explore the small area of the Sea of Tranquillity around their Lunar Module. Jimmy has read the magazine articles, he knows what it took to launch those two men on their 250,000 mile trip, and he is aware how deadly the lunar surface is. It's so very different to the book he finished only last week, with its near-magical substance that cancels out gravity and carries its inventor and his companion to the Moon...

But what's that?

Some flicker of movement off to one side, behind Armstrong. The astronaut shuffles about, turning away from the television camera. Aldrin is out of view. Something scuttles across the screen. Jimmy straightens, he glances over his shoulder at his parents, worried. When he turns back to the television, he sees more shapes. They look like insects, they scuttle like insects, but they are the same size as the astronauts. They stand upright, and their compound eyes glitter like constellations of stars among the blurry greys of the television picture. They swarm over Armstrong, and up the LM's landing-leg. There are hundreds of them.

The television cuts back to the BBC studio. For one long moment, a monochrome James Burke simply gazes out of the screen, blinking owlishly behind his black-framed glasses. He visibly regains his composure, but the images from the Moon still haunt his gaze. NASA, he tells them, has lost contact with Eagle. Command Module Pilot Michael Collins cannot find the Lunar Module's landing-site from orbit, and is as much in the dark as everyone else. More so, perhaps: the darkness of space, the dark side of the Moon. He is the loneliest human being ever.

When his parents put Jimmy to bed an hour later, little more is known of the fate of Armstrong and Aldrin. Mission Control never regains contact. There is life on the Moon, that much is clear. But is it of the Moon? How can anything have evolved on that lifeless grey orb? They are also very much hostile, and NASA's follow-up lunar missions have been shelved indefinitely. Jimmy lies in his bed but he cannot sleep.

It is the end of a dream and the beginning of a nightmare.

1979

The heat of summer, focused through the two walls of floor-to-ceiling windows, has warmed the air, rendering it stale, and now the gym feels much smaller than it actually is. Four lines of desks, each one four feet from its neighbours, stretch from one end of the room to the other. On each desk is a question sheet and an answer sheet; at each desk is a boy in grey trousers and grey shirt. Each boy is busy with a pen, trapped for two hours in this tepid still air.

Jim glances up from his exam paper and across at the window beside his desk. The worsted trousers he wears are too hot; the prickly material itches against his thighs. He has rolled up the sleeves of his shirt and his answer paper sticks to his forearm. He wants to be out there, on the grass, watching the First XI. Not here in an A-level exam. He looks down at his exam paper. Modern History. *The Cold War: its origins and the reasons for its continuing domination of geopolitics.*

Summer should not be spent gazing enviously out of windows while sitting in classrooms or frowning down at question papers. The days last so long, the sun shines until after nine o'clock at night, and it seems criminal to waste a moment of it. It is too hot for the Cold War.

Jim's concentration is dragged from the trees beckoning in the breeze by a door creaking open. He hears rapid footsteps on the polished-wood floor. He looks up to see Mr Mathis, the chemistry teacher, pass him and approach Mr Jackson, the geography teacher, who is invigilating. Mr Mathis reaches Mr Jackson, bends over and whispers something in his ear. Mr Jackson pales; he jerks his head up, neck rigid. They confer in hissed undertones.

Mr Jackson rises to his feet. He tells the boys to put down their pens, he has important news. Missiles have exploded in America, in Florida and California; it was just on the radio. The British government has asked everyone to take precautions. This could be World War III. Jimmy looks down at his exam paper, absurdly scared that his idle wish has heated up the Cold War.

With a scrape and a clatter, the boys squeeze under their desks. Jim wraps his arms about his knees. He knows the desk is no protection against an ICBM. A nearby nuclear explosion would shatter the gym's windows and send slivers of glass spearing across the room. The boys cower fearfully in their useless shelters.

Ten minutes pass. Fifteen. Jim wonders if the two teachers feel as foolish as he does. Could this be a drill? The door to the gym bangs open. Jim squirms round and sees the headmaster, Mr Greene, sweep into the room. The all clear has been given. No ICBMs were launched. The Doomsday Clock has not reached midnight.

Later, in the television room on the study wing, Jim and his friends, perched on battered sofas and armchairs, watch the evening news. The patrician features of Kenneth Kendall replace the BBC's rolling globe. According to the Americans, the Soviets have also suffered a missile attack.

There is a third enemy: the Moon.

The missiles came from the Moon.

Jim immediately remembers that night ten years ago, and the ghostly images on the twenty-four-inch black-and-white Rediffusion. He thinks of his favourite book, about the Edwardian inventor who travels to the Moon. He rereads it regularly, though it reminds him of that black-and-white nightmare ten years ago.

No one sleeps that night, the dormitory is filled with whispers. Prefects wander through the dark room, but are deaf to the rule-breaking. The next morning, the boys gather for a school assembly. Everyone is dull and listless, as if hungover. Mr Greene explains that examinations will be abandoned. Perhaps later, when things have settled, the dead on both sides of the Iron Curtain tallied, perhaps then they can resit them. For now, the boys are to return to their dormitories to pack. Term is ending early. The staff will call the boys' parents to collect them.

Jim has been looking forward to the summer holiday. It has come sooner than expected but he suspects it will not be a happy vacation.

1989

The flash wakes Captain James Alden, and he's already pulling on shirt and trousers when his squadron sergeant major knocks on the door. He tells the man to enter as he struggles into his sweater. Once Alden is dressed, he follows the WO2 out of the building. By the time he gets to where his Recce Squadron of Scimitar CVR(T) tanks waits, engines rumbling, he has been briefed.

Berlin is no more.

That flash was a rocket from the Moon. The aliens have been bombarding the Earth now for a decade, but they are not the only enemy. For weeks, there have been skirmishes between NATO and Warsaw Pact forces in the woods and fields between Magdeburg and Hannover. 1st The Queen's Dragoon Guards has been stationed in Wolfenbüttel at squadron-strength for three months, and they've been out on recces at least twice a week.

This, however, is something different, not a quick sortie along German country lanes following intelligence from a listening post or spotter plane. Alden strides across to his tank, clambers up onto its hull and then onto the turret. He peers down at his gunner, then lowers himself into the Scimitar's interior. Once he's seated and his helmet on, he tells the squadron to move out.

The roar of the Scimitars' Jaguar engines beats off the walls of the Northampton Barracks' blocks, and Alden is grateful for the headphones incorporated into his helmet. The Scimitar lurches into motion, accelerates along the narrow road towards the main gate, and drives out onto Salzdahlumer Straße. The squadron turns left, heading out of Wolfenbüttel and into the countryside.

The Jaguar J60 4.2 litre engines push the eight-tonne Scimitars along at forty kph. The tanks can manage twice that speed, but there's little reason to hurry. Berlin, or what is left of it, is due east of Wolfenbüttel and the horizon in that direction is dominated by a vast cloud mushrooming high into the bright German morning. It's not an unfamiliar sight – Alden has seen similar on the news many times – but this is the closest he has ever been to a strike from the Moon.

The squadron is out among the fields now. From his vantage point in the commander's hatch, Alden is above the hedgerows and can see crops begin to bend in the wind blowing from Berlin. He orders his tanks to disperse. One troop takes the road north to the village of Salzdahlum, and two troops head south to Wendesse and thence to Denkte. His troop heads through Ahlum, along the road to Schöppenstedt.

These are narrow country roads, just like the ones back in the UK, and the Scimitars fill it with their blocky armoured hulls. As they roar past village houses, he sees the residents out on the street, standing by their gates, most in nightclothes and hastily drawn-on coats, staring east at the column of cloud. The rising sun glows through the billowing mass, as if the entire horizon is on fire. The wind is starting to pick up now and it's a hot wind redolent of the fires of hell.

Alden drops down into the turret and slams shut the hatch above him. At Schöppenstedt, the troop turns north-east towards Helmstedt and the border with East Germany. The miles thunder past, the Scimitars jerking about corners, barrelling through the dark forest between Schöppenstedt and Räbke.

This close to the DDR, the squadron observes radio silence as a matter of course. Not, Alden suspects, that anyone has much to say. Berlin, one of the great capitals of the world, is now a crater.

When the Scimitars roar into Helmstedt, the roads are deserted, the town seemingly abandoned. A fierce wind blows rubbish along empty streets, bows the tree-tops, and sets signposts swaying. The tanks bounce onto the autobahn and turn towards Checkpoint Alpha.

Through his periscope, Alden spots a mob of uniformed men walking along the road. He recognises them as East German border guards, Grenztruppen. Over a thousand were stationed at Checkpoint Alpha, and it looks like most of them are walking away from their posts. Into West Germany.

Are they defecting?

The Scimitar slews to a halt across two lanes of the autobahn. The turret traverses left to cover the approaching Grepos. The other three tanks of Alden's troop follow suit, entirely blocking the road. Alden cracks opens the hatch and pokes out his head.

The Grepos have stumbled to a halt, their hands held above their heads. They hunch their shoulders against the gale from the right, against the condemnation they will no doubt receive for deserting their posts, for seeking asylum in the 'decadent' FDR. Alden wonders how long this can go on, how long they will fight each other, while the aliens on the Moon chip away at human civilisation with their rockets. It seems the worst kind of foolishness that the Cold War has continued unabated since the destruction of Cape Kennedy and Baikonur Cosmodrome.

Perhaps this mob of border guards is the first sign of a thaw. Perhaps the baleful wind blowing out of Berlin will warm relations between NATO and the Warsaw Pact.

Perhaps the two great power blocs of planet Earth will finally turn their attention to their common enemy.

1999

The city of Sheffield has been destroyed several times in fiction, but the Moon-dwellers have done a much more effective job of it. Hitting the Earth at more than 25,000 miles an hour, the kinetic warheads of their missiles exploded with one thousand times more energy than the atom bombs which fell on Nagasaki and Hiroshima. The seven hills which ring Sheffield confined the blast, digging a deep crater which was subsequently filled by the River Don. The Steel City is now a lake.

Alden stands on a hill overlooking the placid waters and is reminded of a boyhood trip to the Lake District. But there are no dinghies scudding across Don Lake, no bright triangles of canvas dotting the sluggish waves. The slopes of the hillsides leading down to the lakeshore are hummocked where buildings once stood; and that is where Alden and his team must dig. Buried somewhere under the hillocky ground, in the rubble on which has grown grass, gorse, ash, birch, bramble, in amongst the remains of what was eight years ago a city of half a million people... is buried treasure. Palladium, silver, rhodium, iridium, copper, nickel, cadmium. Plastics which have not biodegraded and can be recycled.

This is what Alden does now, has done since he left the Army six years ago. He mines destroyed cities for scarce materials. There are many like him throughout the world, picking through the ruins of the past two decades to feed the industries of modern society.

The population of the Earth is only a fifth of what it was before, and much more widely dispersed. It is also booming. Low environmental-impact industries maintain a high standard of living. Armies have been scaled back to a few hundred soldiers each since their common enemy is untouchable.

Alden descends the hill to the lakeside, stumbling a little on the mounds and hummocks. The area beneath his feet was once offices and they likely contained computers, printers and other high tech equipment. The computers will be mangled remains now, hard to even identify, but their constituent metals and plastics can be recovered. He kicks listlessly at a tussock of grass, and looks up. It is a cloudless day and a ghost Moon hangs over the lake. It is pale and insubstantial, washed out by the sunshine. It looks the same as ever, though the war between the two planets is twenty years old.

Alden has heard the Americans are putting together a force to strike back. He wants in: he served in the Army for eleven years and he knows he has the necessary skills.

This could be his last treasure hunt, he thinks. He tries not to dwell on the bodies that lie beneath his feet, the five hundred thousand who died when Sheffield was destroyed. All the same he feels a need to strike back in the name of those countless dead.

He wonders how the Americans plan to travel to the Moon. They have no launch pads for rockets: the Moon-dwellers would target anything which resembled one. Perhaps the Americans have invented anti-gravity, or discovered some substance with that property, as in his favourite novel, the one he rereads every few years. It might well be such a breakthrough which has prompted the plan to attack the Moon.

Or the Americans could have, he supposes, built rockets secretly in underground launch facilities, like something out of a James Bond film. If he remembers rightly, one film featured a rocket launching from inside a volcano. A fake roof disguised as a lake hid the launch pad, a lake much like this one he stands beside.

But Don Lake is real, he can hear it lapping leadenly against the muddy shore, can see that the breeze keeps the surface in constant motion. Alden turns about and gazes up the hill to where his team waits. The sooner they get started, the better.

He wants this finished, and then he will be free to volunteer for the invasion of the Moon.

2009

Two hundred aeroplanes fly in formation across the Atlantic at forty thousand feet. Just south of Greenland, two hundred boosters slide backwards from beneath the bellies of the aircraft. The rockets drop vertically towards the sea. The sky is filled with falling cylinders of polished metal as, above them, the two hundred planes bank sharply for the flight home. As one, two hundred rocket engines ignite. Their roar fills the heavens.

In a Crew Module atop one of the boosters, Lieutenant-Colonel James Alden watches the instrument panel before him. Acceleration pushes him deeper into his chair. The screens and readouts display flight data, but it means little to him. He is a soldier, not a pilot. The rocket is flown entirely by computer. The eight soldiers inside the CM have no way of controlling it.

The acceleration holds steady at three Gs. Alden suffers in silence. He hears a muffled bang as the first stage, now spent, disengages and falls away. A sudden punch between his shoulder blades tells him the second stage has lit. Moments later, they are in orbit. A funereal silence fills the Crew Module. Someone gives a nervous cough.

A grinding noise, followed by a clunk, sounds from the rear. It is repeated. Both solar panel arrays have successfully opened.

Alden turns to the horizon window beside him. He can see the Earth, a nacreous blue. It appears to be above him, a ceiling bowed beneath its own weight. Hanging from it like a child's mobile is a formation of two hundred silver teardrops. As one, the spacecraft initiate Trans Lunar Injection: flame bursts from their engine-bells and, slowly but with increasing speed, the formation moves out of Earth orbit.

Three days later, the cratered monochrome face of the Moon now fills the window by Alden's head. He and his section are ready in their spacesuits, helmets sealed and life-support system backpacks plugged in. The Crew Module shakes as it disengages from its Service Module. The view through the window swings dizzily from the Moon's pitted grey to the black of space. The CM, atop its descent stage, falls towards the lunar surface.

The Crew Module pitches up once again, and now Alden can see the lunar horizon. It rises up the window as the spacecraft descends. Moments later, his view is obscured by dust. The CM hatch blows with a loud bang. Air rushes out, taking sound with it; but the soldiers are held firm in their seats.

Once the interior is in vacuum, the lighting switches to red. Alden unbuckles his straps and struggles clumsily to his feet. In the one-sixth gravity and bulky spacesuit, he finds it difficult to move in the cramped interior. He steps up to the open hatchway, and finds himself looking over a forest of silver spacecraft planted in a plain of featureless black and grey.

He jumps down. Dust puffs up about his boots; and then falls with strange suddenness. Someone barks orders over the radio. Alden turns back to his CM, and one of his soldiers hands him his rifle. He gathers his section behind him and, with a curt order for them to follow, begins to kangaroo-hop across the lunar surface.

As they approach the entrance to the Moon-dwellers' underground hive, Alden spots something odd: a splash of colour in the monochrome rim of a crater. He puts up a hand and brings his section to a halt. With a series of leaps, he approaches the object.

It is a book, bound in red leather, sitting half buried in the regolith. He cannot bend over in his spacesuit, so he carefully scrapes his boot across the cover until he has cleared away the grey dust and revealed its title: *The Complete Works of Shakespeare.*

Alden looks across at the task force, sixteen hundred figures in white spacesuits, leaping silently across the lunar plain amid a cloud of grey dust. He considers reporting his find. No, he decides: he came here, flew a quarter of a million miles across space, to take the fight to the enemy. He will not jeopardise that. He signals for his section to continue onto the hive entrance.

Inside the cave-like opening, the passage is wide and smooth, but not high. Now they must shuffle along, kicking up the lunar dust, which falls swiftly to the floor and does not obscure their way. The tunnel opens out and Alden halts. Ahead are half a dozen figures. Moon-dwellers. It is his first clear sight of them. They are some five feet tall, and appear to be clad in stiff leathery material. On their heads they wear many-spiked helmets, with goggles of dark glass set on either side. They have long whip-like antenna and short, flimsy legs. They do not appear to be carrying weapons.

Alden fires his assault rifle. The Moon-dwellers are silently cut apart by bullets. He does not know if his section is shooting too, he can hear only his breath harsh in his helmet.

Alden remembers two men in spacesuits not unlike the one he now wears. He recalls a small boy who sat before a twenty-four inch black-and-white Rediffusion and watched in horror as his dreams were destroyed. He thinks of cities smashed and their populations slaughtered, and he wonders at the motives of the Moon-dwellers... And he rues that humanity's response should be this, as he moves forward... into the Unknown – into the dark, into the silence that has no end...

'The Clever Skeleton' is a wonderful example of how much resonance can be achieved even with the very shortest of stories.

The Clever Skeleton

James Collett

A skeleton floated past Jim's bedroom window, horizontally outstretched, cruising through the night, and turned its head as it passed, so as to look Jim squarely in the eye.

Being four years old, Jim did not recognise the incident as his first hallucination: instead he concluded that a skeleton – and one possessed of some surprising liveliness – was taking a personal interest in his affairs. Jim was puzzled, but carried on with his child's life, having no choice in the matter, and went to playschool and ate with plastic cutlery and learned new words.

Soon he noticed that there was a presence, just behind him, wherever he went. He learned the word *follow*. He understood that the skeleton was following him. It always knew Jim's next move, and was always able to keep behind him. Jim could never about-turn quickly enough to catch a glimpse of the skeleton. It was too fast. It was as lithe as they come, dancing like a boxer to keep out of Jim's sight.

At night, the skeleton hid under Jim's bed, but when Jim ducked his head down to look under there, the skeleton slid out, bright as can be, and crept up the other side of the bed, unseen. The skeleton was clever. Jim learned the word *invisible*. The skeleton was visible only to Jim, and so it needed only to hide from him. Jim learned the word *hallucination*. He had known, before he'd learnt the word *hallucination*, that he should not tell anyone about the skeleton.

When Jim grew up, he drank a lot of beer, and grew fond of solitude and rainstorms. He no longer tried to catch the skeleton. He sat or stood in the quietest places he could find, drinking beer and hoping for rain, and it was as if the skeleton was drinking and hoping, too. Jim understood that he did not know where he was going any more than the skeleton knew why it was following him there.

The skeleton followed Jim to work and stood behind him while he wrapped sandwiches, worked cash registers, sliced cold meats, labelled products, painted houses, pulled pints, dug gardens, delivered magazines, washed windows, and swept floors. It followed him to jobcentres, council offices, hospitals, bus stations, bars, and all around the houses. They went up and down the country together, for reasons neither of them knew.

I am the clever skeleton. I follow him around – this guy, Jim – and I don't let him see me, though he knows I'm here. I stay three steps behind him when he's walking and peer over his shoulder when he's not; and sometimes, if he happens to do or see something interesting, I take a break from him. I stop somewhere, while he carries on walking, and I write down what he's done or seen, and then I find him again. He always seems to have cheered up a little by the time I catch up with him.

I still haven't entirely made up my mind what's happening in the following atmospheric and curious story from Tony Lovell. Or maybe I have.

The Stairwell

Tony Lovell

The girl is on the stairwell in another unfashionable dress: hiding from the rain, Colin guesses. He feels her looking down on him as he climbs up towards her.

'Jill,' he says, not liking how out of breath he sounds.

She never acknowledges him with a greeting but rather something interesting, a story or question, some strange idea. He looks forward to it, but always feels self conscious listening to her alone out here.

'Someone keeps visiting us,' she says today.

'A friend? A relative?'

He regrets this last word. But she lets it go.

'No. Someone from the future.'

He doesn't laugh. 'Who?'

'A woman. I don't know her. I'm trying to find her.'

She leans over the metal rail, looks up and down into the dust, the grey concrete and iron rails. She and Colin are halfway up; it looks endless. 'Are you still scared of the lift?' she says.

'Yes, a little,' Colin says. 'But I do prefer the stairs. I like being able to see things. And they keep me fit. What makes you think it's a woman?'

Jill rests her pointed chin on the heels of her hands. She looks much older for a moment, falsely wise. 'I can't explain it.'

Colin is carrying a bag of shopping in each hand. There are eggs in one of them and they feel like the heaviest things because of their fragility. He shifts them one from one hand to the other, the pain lessening even though the bags are just about the same weight as each other.

She is a lovely girl, Jill. He thinks it is the atmosphere of the tower that makes her this way, tolerant of her elders, the only child living in the place. She reminds him of Marcia, makes him feel he's back in the days when he knew her.

A door opens deep downstairs but doesn't close again. Someone listening. 'I have to go,' he says. 'Let me know if you find her.'

The Gardeners are coming at four. Colin makes himself a black tea while he waits and looks down from his window to the road that goes into the city at the bottom of the valley. They are coming from miles away, and because of this he supposes they will as likely as not never use him. He hopes the sense of pointlessness does not show if and when they arrive, and hopes also, sadly, that they do not use him; even if he does need their money.

At ten past four they ring, asking for directions. He sees what must be their car muddling round the roads at the foot of the flats and feels suddenly sorry for them: they look like children, playing at being grown-ups.

'We're sorry,' the mother says when they get there. 'We tried to squeeze in a meal in town.'

'Which town? There are two.'

She tells him.

She leaves him with her fidgety, gangly son and vacant-looking Dad, who defers every decision to her, like someone just out of prison or hospital. 'I'm helping a friend move a bed,' she says. 'My husband can't drive.'

Dad winces.

For an awkward near-hour they do a few sums to suss out how capable the boy is. Dad tries the sums, too, and it dawns on Colin that he will be absorbing some of his son's work for himself. 'You should be able to sit the exam in a year,' he tells them, both of them.

They seem more pleased than they should be. Something feels to be going on, but Colin is unable to pinpoint what.

'Can my son look out of your window?' Dad asks. The boy is seventeen; it seems a juvenile request. The boy does not seem embarrassed.

'Feel free,' Colin says.

They look, and look, like they've never seen a town before, or been more than two floors up above the ground. 'It reminds me of the flats I lived in as a kid,' Dad says, eventually. 'Same fittings and everything.' He smiles, like he must have a Marcia too.

'It's all adults here,' Colin says. 'Old people, mostly. Bachelors, spinsters, widows.'

'We saw a girl in the entrance.'

'Jill. She's only one. Her mother died. Her grandparents have her here through the week while her father works. She's no bother.'

'She must get lonely.'

The boy doesn't say a word. He is held by the window, one of his hands twisting a piece of red string that hangs from the pocket of a coat he hasn't taken off during the whole of the hour.

Time drags, a conversation never quite forms. When they leave earlier than they said they would, Dad says, 'We'll ring.'

Colin has never thought about Jill's loneliness before. She has never seemed it. He realises that she is living pretty much as he does, entertaining herself, and it is why he has not noticed, or given it thought. She always seems so bright, content.

One day during a rainy Easter holiday he bumps into her on the stairs again, all lively, saying 'I've seen her.'

It has been weeks since they last met like this. It feels like months, but also no time at all.

'Go on,' he says.

'You won't laugh? You'll believe me?'

'I always believe you.'

She looks around, her eyes half closed, like she is trying to picture what happened. 'She was here, on the stairs, a couple of floors up. She was young, not like the other people that live here. I felt her looking down on me. When I looked up I saw her hair – yellow it was, like mine – and her funny clothes. In fact it was her clothes made me think she was joking with me.'

'She said she was from the future? She really said that?'

'Yes. And I do believe her. She liked everything too much. She said she was looking for something too, but that if she told me it would spoil it.'

'How long was she here? And when?'

'Not long. It was last week. Ages ago.'

Lonely, yes, after all. Imagining things too vividly to be healthy. So innocent.

'So she wasn't looking for you?'

The girl seems flustered by this. Her eyes flicker and her words become stuck. 'I, I don't think so.'

He has said something frightening. 'You wouldn't want to go to the future with her, would you?'

She looks down the well. 'I'm not sure. I think it would frighten me. Just the going would frighten me, not where it might end up.'

'What would you do, if she asked?'

'I don't know.'

She puts her palm to her forehead. He wishes she didn't look like she's making it up. 'Has she described the future?'

'She said it was only a little different. She said it was safer in ways but more dangerous, too. She said people were largely unhappy but that there were less problems. There was a lot of old stuff about, she said, they had to use lots of old things, things we have now and think of as new.'

He presses her for answers, perhaps a little too much. There's a danger of forcing invention.

'She said these days look like scenery to her. There were things she'd forgotten; seeing them brought back memories. She was here before, when she was very little.'

She looks at him, up from the rail. 'You don't believe me, do you?'

'It's hard to. I can't see how she can do it. I don't think I can believe in time travel.'

He feels sad admitting this, as if over all his years he has been lying to himself.

'She didn't use a machine,' Jill says. 'She said anyone can do it, that she discovered how to by accident.'

Her hair hangs down into the stairwell, the rail digging into her bare armpits, the most worn and lined part of her.

'Did she describe how she did it?'

She opens her mouth to form a word but then the door below them opens with a clacking that echoes up and down for ages, and Mrs Tabor looks up at them. 'You can get kicked out for this,' she says, 'making a racket.' She's trying to make it light, like she's joking, but it doesn't ring true.

'I'm sorry, Mrs Tabor. Jill was telling me a story. A good one.'

'A true one,' the girl says, casting Colin a hurt look.

'She always is,' Mrs Tabor says.

Her husband is not long dead. Her fuse has shortened.

That is a thing with the flats. It's all little encounters, meetings in corridors and halls, outside of doors. So many short fuses always making him wince, but he understands them, knows where they come from.

Mrs Tabor offers him tea to make up for her fuse; she doesn't invite Jill. 'She's lonely,' he tells her, 'she loves having a chat.'

'Strange rubbish she talks, though.'

'But entertaining.'

The kettle blows, an old-fashioned whistle.

There are things of Mr Tabor's still around the now half-empty flat: his coat on the back of the door, a tobacco tin on top of the gas fire mantelpiece, a pair of slippers with fuzzy toes and holes where his heels had buried into the soles curled up under a chair.

'Everybody likes her,' Colin says.

The woman tries to straighten a crease on the curtains with her fingers, casts a brief look into the valley.

The flat is the same shape as Colin's; it faces the same way but is two floors below. It is not a bit like it in any other respect: it feels smaller, crammed with ornaments and decorations that poke out to form a kind of grotto. Flowered walls, flowered sofa with legs instead of castors, a glass cabinet filled with glasses and porcelain animals. On top of it all and on the wall above the cabinet are a series of photographs of a young man gradually growing; Colin has never seen him before. 'She says we have a time traveller,' he says.

'Yes, I heard. I think she's having her on, though. Humouring her.'

A simple thing then, most likely an ordinary thing. 'You've seen the woman?'

'No. Just heard. You can't see properly through that glass.' She puts the silver tray down in front of them: china cups and saucers as dainty as something from a doll's house, a little bowl filled half-up with sugar, a plate of biscuits. 'I feel bad cutting her short like that,' she says. 'I don't know why I did. I thought she might have been bothering you.'

He wants to press on about the mystery woman on the stairs, but instead says, 'Jill's no trouble. She livens things up, makes a change.'

The woman is perhaps no more than fifteen years older than him but could be his grandmother. The flat is even very much like his grandmother's bungalow back in Newcastle, as comforting to him as it had once been. 'Have you been alright here?' he says.

'I'm trying to see people. People have been very nice but they can only manage it so long. I think I make them sad. I don't mean to.'

The man nods. A silence comes, a sense of embarrassment. 'Yes. I've become dull these days. And unsightly. You feel like you'd be best off in a cupboard, sometimes.'

'We sort of are, up here.'

She keeps looking at the window, but he realises it's the little crease in the curtain that's bothering her. Her tension about it rubs off on him and he feels it's time to go.

It is a long time since he has sat and talked with anyone like this in their home. Neither has he talked in a pub or café.

He wonders when it happened, the first trickling out of life, and it's with dismay he realises he might never have really entered it in the first place.

His own flat sometimes feels different after he's been with people. Tonight he finds himself looking over his shoulder, closing doors and opening them again. He doesn't know why he feels frightened because no one has said or done anything frightening. But it doesn't stop him putting on the big light instead of the little lamp while he listens to the news, leaving the curtains open on the two ordinary cities and all their lights.

Certain books bothered him like this as a child, excited him too much. The substance of reality felt soft, pliant, infused with possibility and meaning. He was the kind of child to believe toys were real and moved when you left the room, to hang on too long to the idea of Santa being a real person.

In bed he tosses and turns, stares over at the door he's left open before getting up and closing it, wedging it with a spy book he's been trying and failing to read.

The family have not got back to him. It makes him miserable even though he knew it would happen, half hoped for it. Somewhere there is a plan for such times as this on a piece of paper: 'Living Life to the Full', a list of procedures to ensure the smooth-going of things. He was supposed to have filled it in weeks ago but hasn't: his problems felt inconsequential when it came to recording them in print, something that had probably been the point of it.

And yet, the funny thing is, he is not thoroughly miserable: it's the thing with Jill and her 'future friend', things like that, his imagination keeping him rolling. He has haunted the stairs hoping to glimpse this 'future friend', listening at the knobbly glass when he's out on the landing. He does his shopping every day instead of every week for bits and bobs, enjoying the exercise and seeing people, buying things just outside their sell-by dates, letting chance govern his variety.

But there is definitely a hollow that cannot be filled with imaginings or treats or change. It is in all the stair-haunting, the waiting for a look from a set of eyes that know how things will turn out.

'You seem distracted,' Mrs Tabor says one day. 'Like you've lost something.'

The spoons for the sugar are all tarnished. They have a flattened Buddha at the end. He has not had tea with sugar since his teens, he realises. Stirring it in makes the china ring like a little silver bell, takes him back to more certain times.

She looks at him sideways while she cuts open a packet of bourbons. 'Are you wondering where she is?' she says.

'Who?'

'Marcia.'

'Don't you mean – ?' He stops himself. 'Have I ever talked about Marcia?'

'Only once or twice.'

He wonders if it's true, for he doesn't feel as if he has. It is possible: she is never far from his mind, what with living here in the flats and it all being so very similar.

'She was a girl I knew for maybe two or three days,' he said. 'I must have been about ten years old. She lived in a house in Newcastle down the road from an old aunt we used to visit, and I can't remember how we got talking, but we did. Like children do, I suppose.'

He had not known about love, he realises. He wonders if it was what he had felt for her, what things felt like when you did not have the vocabulary with which to pin them down.

Suddenly the woman reaches over and does a puzzling and very intimate thing, takes his hands in hers and looks down at them like she might somehow read something in them. 'You ever feel you know what's coming?' she says, making the feeling almost certain.

'Never,' he says. 'But I do wonder about it.'

'That's not the same,' she says. Then she looks up and out and down the bank, or maybe at the crease again. He cannot see the silver trickle where the two cities meet: he has never needed to since those first, haunting times.

'Have you ever been on the top floor?' he says.

'I've been in the Whites' flat, the next floor down. They left, had a son. And Beryl Ernshaw. Why'd you ask?'

'The view changes with every floor you go on. Different parts of the city visible from each. I think how it feels like we probably haven't met everyone here, sometimes, even though we think we have. In your mind it doesn't feel like many people live here, really. You wouldn't be sure if you bumped into someone that they were a stranger.'

Was this too much? Should the words have stayed thoughts?

'There was a cough in that corridor once,' she says, finger pointing over his shoulder. 'Mr Tabor was out and I was in on my own. It was just outside that door behind you, clear as day.' She looks up at it as if to verify it. 'It didn't frighten me because it sounded so real and ordinary. At least not till I asked who it was and there wasn't an answer.'

'This place is full of little noises, if you listen. You almost don't have to put the telly on.'

The bent woman looks hurt. 'I'm sure my cough wasn't in my mind.'

Colin says nothing. He sinks into the armchair supping his tea, running his thumb over the silver Buddha. He is thinking about Marcia again, now he's been prompted, and the flats on Westgate road, her little house behind the shops. How long had he known her, he wonders? How many times had he gone to visit her? With some dismay he realises it must have amounted to no more than four or five times, but all of them intense visits playing with plastic animals in the yard, making a little zoo out of matchboxes, burying a dead blackbird under a tree. He had not known many girls. He would carry the fact to his grave.

'You're away again,' Mrs Tabor says, and there is more tea, another ring of a bell.

He goes walking one night, leaves his flat and climbs the tower in the dark. The place is all old dinner smells and rippling reflections on tiled landings, not even a murmur behind any of the doors.

From the top stairwell he looks down on the cities, their golden light. The stairwells themselves feel busy with the sounds of his footsteps and straining breaths. At the top of each are those mysterious doors he's never seen the other sides of that lead up onto the roof, black and flat with the only detail the keyholes, always too dark to see anything through.

He hadn't expected to meet anyone but he does.

He feels like hugging her when he sees her. She is like blood out of a stone. 'She asked me what you said,' she says, 'that did I want to go with her.'

The news of her meeting the woman is almost enough to stop his sadness. 'What did you say?'

'I said I might go for a while. See what it's like.'

'And?'

'She told me how to get back. And that it could go wrong, that I had to understand that.'

There is a shape in the dust. She rolls it with the tip of her toe, back and forth till it becomes firm, then pushes it down into the well where it falls lightly down like a feather. 'I've tried to see her,' he says, 'looking round here at night. But I haven't even heard her.'

'She needs to come to you. She has the *things*, you see...'

Jill feels different. Something has happened to her. But he can't say what. 'Has she said why she wants you? Do you really think it's safe?'

'She says it's safer than here.'

Colin looks down into the well, worried they are talking too loudly and might be interrupted.

'She thinks I'm lonely. I'm too much for Nan and Granddad, my dad.'

'Isn't there really anyone else?'

The dust mouse gone, she moves her toes, scratching circles in the ground.

'We all worry about you,' he says. 'I was an only child, like you. But I never felt lonely. You have your imagination, you see, when you're like us. It's kind of a friend to you.'

She has such big brown eyes, almost as bulging as Marcia's had been, and the same boy-shaped, skinny body. Her slender hand reaches out and drops something warm and hard into his.

'This is one of the things she gave me,' she says, 'to help me get there.'

It is a coin.

Colin tilts it back and forward, feels it with his hard fingertips. It is difficult to see it out here at this side of the flats, the sun sinking down at the other. 'It's not a token, is it? From the garage or the bingo?'

She shakes her head.

I must be ill, after all, he thinks, falling for a child's game like this. 'Is it for me?' he says.

'No,' she says. 'It's to get me there. You need five things, she said, to travel through time: a sound, a smell, a taste, a thing, and a memory. But if you have a person you don't need any of them. They have everything, you see.'

Colin leans back against the wall, a little dizzy. 'Yes,' he says, 'I can understand it.'

The sun must be dipping beneath the horizon. The place was dark. In a minute or two the lights would come on and she would stop being so indistinct.

'She tells me in the dark, holds my hand,' she says, 'tells me what the future is like. I feel like I'm halfway there sometimes, when she tells me: her clothes smell funny, different. I need to tell people I'm going, she said, but try not to upset them, just be nice. Not a proper word goodbye you understand, but rather something that makes them realise later and not feel so bad.'

The wonder in Colin changes. Something dark dawns on him. 'Maybe you're just imagining yourself into those places,' he says. 'Thinking hard or something.'

The girl lowers her face. 'There needs to be a bridge, she said. To someone you know well. It doesn't work if they're not there. It'd just be daydreaming.'

She rests a hand on his arm, awkwardly, like she's been told to rather than wants to.

The restlessness will never go away, he realises. In a day or so he will even see her again and her story will be silly, and there will be nothing wrong with that. It won't be disappointing, if it's false. Just how she is.

After leaving her he goes upstairs and makes a cup of tea, turns on the radio, immersing himself in the current. He can still feel her hand on his arm and it bothers him and he rubs it, only it comes back: the feeling is not in his arm, not really.

Down in the valley the roads run into the cities like water. He gives them a glance and turns off the radio, puts on the television for the noise and colour, the faces. Upstairs a chair drags over lino. Another channel comes on up there, different to his own, and he switches his television off again to listen to it, figure out what it might be. It is too late now to go downstairs and see Mrs Tabor.

The last of our flash fiction pieces comes from relative newcomer Damon King.

SIMMO!

Damon King

The Evening Herald was full of praise for Dean Simmons. He was bright. He was popular. He was an aspiring footballer. Well, I happened to know him. The lad was a little shit who picked on me every day on my way to school. And I don't care what people say, just because he is dead doesn't change a thing. As far as I'm concerned there was nothing bright about him tearing my schoolbag from my shoulder and emptying my PE kit into the stream at the end of Brynland Avenue. And there was nothing popular about him clipping my heels so that I tripped over myself in front of all the girls from Class 3H.

The night of the accident, I remember coming home to find Mum and Auntie Christine muttering and whispering in the kitchen about how awful it all was. I lost count of how many times they used the word 'tragic'. How such a young man shouldn't really have been whizzing around on a motorbike, especially with the snow and ice on the roads. The news had been full of pictures of people spinning the wheels of their cars in an attempt to overcome the merest of inclines, or even just to pull away from the kerb. Despite Mum's incessant tutting, Dad and I were in hysterics of laughter watching people fall onto their backsides.

The thing is, I knew a couple of things that Mum and Auntie Christine didn't. Fact one: Dean wasn't even old enough to be riding that motorbike. Fact two: the bike was stolen. To be more accurate, it wasn't a stolen *bike*: it was made up of parts from numerous stolen *bikes*, all taken by Dean. Despite his ability to charm his elders and give the appearance of being a nice, respectable young man, I knew that he was no more than a petty thief. He had been threatening me and robbing my dinner money for the last two school terms, and now I think about it, that probably amounts to over two hundred pounds.

As for the claim that he was an aspiring footballer, well, that's pure fiction. For sure, he was in the school team, but everybody knew that to be in the school team you just had to turn up at the pitch and Mr Trevis would be delighted. The fact was, we barely had eleven decent players in our year. But once you travelled up to St Mary's Boys' Club, there were dozens of players better than Dean. I vividly remember watching one game when Kevin Cantwell played the ball through Dean's legs and then turned straight around and nutmegged him again, just to humiliate him. So, if by 'aspiring', the *Herald* meant that maybe, possibly, one day, he could become a good player, then we'll never know, but judging by the fact that he struggled to get into St Mary's second team, I very much doubt it.

You see, I think these newspapers, especially local ones, are so desperate for a story sometimes, that when a youngster dies they automatically try to portray the deceased in a great light. Don't get me wrong, sometimes they are an aspiring this, or an aspiring that. David LaCroix was an aspiring ballroom dancer, and when his body was found in the quarry late on that summer's evening the papers were correct in describing him so. His dad had been French national ballroom champion and he had pushed David to the point that he made the British Juniors. Now that is what I call aspiring, whereas I would put Dean in a category with the likes of Stevey Norris and Omar Hakim. To my disbelief, they were also painted as local heroes, but it couldn't have been further from the truth: they received their fatal injuries while trying to steal the lead cladding from the roof of Backdell Community Centre, for God's sake!

We'll never see it, but if it is a journalist's duty to tell the truth, then it would be refreshing to see an article stating that the deceased will not be missed in the slightest as he, or she, was a complete pain in the arse. I have always been taught that honesty is the best policy.

Now, this is where I find myself in a bit of a quandary: I haven't been completely honest myself. When Mum asked me about Dean, I made sure to sing his praises. The thing is, I couldn't really be seen to be slagging him off.

There was another thing that Mum and Auntie Christine didn't know. Fact three: On the night in question, I had spotted Dean pulling out of the side street – not Dawson Close, the other one, a little further up by the car park – I think it's called Mayfair or Mayflower or something similar. He was trying to cross over into the lane heading up the main road. He had to wait for a short time, until the lights slowed the traffic heading in the opposite direction. As he couldn't see me stood behind the wheelie bins next to the chip shop, I had time to gather some snow and compact it into an icy ball. I kept one eye on the lights and then, as he rounded the corner, I gave a quick shout of 'Simmo!' before launching it with all my pent-up hatred in his direction. I couldn't have known that my throw would be so accurate. The ball wedged itself in his half-open visor and he started to lose balance immediately. He did his best to maintain his direction, but the ice was causing his rear tyre to spin and flail in increasingly exaggerated swings like the tail of a fish being pulled from the water, and before I knew it, he was half toppled over. His knee hit the ground and caused him to be pulled around and under those massive black tyres.

The driver must have been too distracted by the snow flurries being whipped across his windscreen to have noticed why Dean lost his balance. For days I watched the local news like a hawk to make sure that no foul play was suspected.

Do I feel guilty? Well, believe me, I'm not completely heartless, but one thing's for sure: Dean Simmons was a little shit, and no obituary or sparkling write-up in the *Evening Herald* will ever change that.

About the Contributors

Gavin Cameron has been writing since 2010, mainly under the tutorship of author Zöe Venditozzi. He writes short stories and flash fiction on a variety of themes, and has three unpublished novels. He volunteers at a hospital radio station.

James Collett is 28, very skint, quite bitter, and good at rolling cigarettes. He lives, mostly on beans, in Cheltenham, and has never had any failed marriages, nor any successful ones. He retired from shelf-stacking and alcoholism a year ago and now writes full-time for almost no money. He never does anything useful.

Cindy George was first published as a writer of short stories for *Just Seventeen* magazine in the late eighties, and as a music journalist for the *NME* and others in the fallow period between acid house and Britpop. She worked in radio advertising for many years, and has also been a press officer and a farmhand on a banana plantation. She has an MA in Writing from Warwick University, and is working on her first novel.

Tania Hershman is the author of two story collections: *My Mother Was An Upright Piano: Fictions* (Tangent Books, 2012), a collection of 56 very short fictions, and *The White Road and Other Stories* (Salt, 2008; commended, 2009 Orange Award for New Writers).

Andrew Jury was born and lives in Leicester, England, and works part-time for a health and safety company. He's been writing for over twenty years, and had stories appear in *Cemetery Dance*, *Lighthouse 5* and an anthology of speculative fiction, *Dark Doorways*.

He also has a story due for publication in a forthcoming issue of *Postscripts*. Andrew's especially influenced by, and in awe of, many post-war US writers, most notably Tobias Wolff, Richard Ford and "the late, great John Cheever".

Damon King has been writing short stories for less than a year. To date, as well as 'Simmo!', he has one other published story in *Knife Edge: An Anthology of Crime, Thriller, Mystery and Suspense*.

He has a number of other stories that he hopes to publish in one form or another.

Tim Lay has worked as a journalist, builder's mate, TEFL teacher and inventor of card games. His debut novel, *The*

Sewerside Chronicles, won the Undiscovered Authors prize in 2007. He runs Brighton literary night Grit Lit.

Paul Lenehan lives, works and writes in Dublin. Publication credits for 2013 include short stories in the journal *Philosophy Now* in the UK and, in Ireland, *The Clifden Anthology 2013* and *Crannóg* magazine. He has just this year completed a Honours Maths degree with the Open University.

Tony Lovell writes only occasionally, but has appeared in *All Hallows*, *Supernatural Tales*, as well as various anthologies by Terry Grimwood and D F Lewis. His story for The Fiction Desk represents his first step into mainstream(ish!) literature.

S R Mastrantone is a writer and musician from Birmingham, now living in Oxford. His stories have been published or are forthcoming in *Lamplight, Carte Blanche, Stupefying Stories* and *The Waterhouse Review*. He is currently working on his first novel. When he isn't writing, he can usually be found conducting rock experiments in his band The Woe Betides.

Matt Plass lives in Sussex. He works in e-learning, previously edited *Tall Tales & Modern Fables* magazine and is one half of Bread and Love Productions.

Matt is making his third Fiction Desk appearance in this volume.

Ian Sales has been published in a number of magazines and original anthologies. In 2012, he edited the original anthology *Rocket Science* for Mutation Books. He founded Whippleshield Books, through which he is publishing his *Apollo Quartet* of literary hard sf novellas. The first book of the quartet, *Adrift on the*

Sea of Rains, was published in April 2012 and won the BSFA Award in the short fiction category for that year. It is also a finalist for the Sidewise Award. The second book, *The Eye With Which The Universe Beholds Itself*, was published in January 2013.

Ian Shine lives in southeast London and works as a sub-editor. His short stories have appeared in *Scraps*, the anthology for National Flash Fiction Day 2013, been shortlisted for the Stork Press mini short story competition, and are due to appear in *Stories for Home*, a collection of stories put together to raise money for homelessness charity Shelter.

Warwick Sprawson is from Melbourne, Australia. While his stories have appeared in many Australian publications, 'The System' is his first story published in the UK. A keen hiker, he also writes travel articles for *Wild*, *Great Walks*, and *Australian Outdoor Geographic*.

Robert Summersgill recently graduated from Bath Spa University with a degree in Creative Writing. He lives in Bath and is writing his first novel. This is his first published story but not his last.

For more information on the contributors
to this volume, please visit our website:

www.thefictiondesk.com/authors

Also from The Fiction Desk:

Various Authors

the first Fiction Desk anthology

These stories will take you from the shores of Lake Garda in Italy to a hospital room in Utah, from a retirement home overlooking the Solent to an unusual school in the wilds of Scotland. Meet people like Daniel, a government employee looking for an escape; and William, a most remarkable dog by anyone's standards.

Various Authors is the first volume in our new series of anthologies dedicated to discovering and publishing the best new short fiction.

New stories by:

Charles Lambert	Matthew Licht
Lynsey May	Ben Lyle
Jon Wallace	Danny Rhodes
Patrick Whittaker	Harvey Marcus
Adrian Stumpp	Alex Cameron
Jason Atkinson	Ben Cheetham

Avilable to order from all good British bookshops, or online at www.thefictiondesk.com.

£9.99

Out now.

ISBN 9780956784308

Also from The Fiction Desk:

All These Little Worlds

the second Fiction Desk anthology

Among the stories in our second anthology: a new dress code causes havoc in an American school, a newspaper mistake leads a retired comedian to look back over a not-quite-spotless career, and a family buys an unusual addition to their fish tank.

This volume also features 'Pretty Vacant', a special long story from Charles Lambert.

New stories by:

Charles Lambert
Jason Atkinson
Halimah Marcus
Andrew Jury
James Benmore
Colin Corrigan
Ryan Shoemaker
Jennifer Moore
Mischa Hiller

Avilable to order from all good British bookshops, or online at www.thefictiondesk.com.

£9.99

Out now.

ISBN 9780956784322

Also from The Fiction Desk:

The Maginot Line

the third Fiction Desk anthology

Our third anthology contains nine new short stories, from debut authors, returning contributors, and authors who are new to us but might be familiar to you. Highlights include journalist Benjamin Johncock's fiction debut, the return of two popular Fiction Desk contributors: Andrew Jury and Harvey Marcus; a new story from SF stalwart Ian Sales; and the title story by Matt Plass.

New stories by:

Benjamin Johncock
Ian Sales
Claire Blechman
Andrew Jury
Harvey Marcus
Matt Plass
Shari Aarlton
Mandy Taggart
Justin D. Anderson

Avilable to order from all good British bookshops,
or online at www.thefictiondesk.com.

£9.99

Out now.

ISBN 9780956784346

Also from The Fiction Desk:

Crying Just Like Anybody

the fourth Fiction Desk anthology

Our fourth anthology takes its title from a story by Richard Smyth, and features ten new stories.

Newcomers to the series include Die Booth, Mike Scott Thomson, William Thirsk-Gaskill, Luiza Sauma and S R Mastrantone.

This volume also features our first story in translation, with 'I'm the One' from Slovenian author Miha Mazzini.

New stories by:

Colin Corrigan	Mike Scott Thomson
S R Mastrantone	Miha Mazzini
Die Booth	William Thirsk-Gaskill
Matthew Licht	Luiza Sauma
Matt Plass	Richard Smyth

Avilable to order from all good British bookshops, or online at www.thefictiondesk.com.

£9.99

Out now.

ISBN 9780956784360